THE SHAMANIC PROPHECY

With best wishes,

Heath

By
Heath Shedlake

Text copyright © 2013 Heath Shedlake
All rights reserved
Published by Heath Shedlake

I would like to express my deep gratitude to Andrejka for her patience and help in editing my manuscript. I would also like to thank Patricia and Liz without whom this would not have been possible. Lastly I would like to thank Derek Murphy for producing and creating a wonderful front cover design.

VENEZUELA 1697

CHAPTER ONE

Jabuti stood on the banks of the mighty Orinoco, leaning against a tree with a slightly distracted air. His piercing blue eyes gazed across its mighty expanse focusing on nothing in particular. Daydreaming, he was interrupted as a formation of toucans flew by, colouring the sky with their vibrant plumage. With the deep throaty calls of howler monkeys calling out to each other he became distracted with their cries, finding them strangely hypnotic and comforting. Soaking up the sights and sounds he felt insignificant within the enormity of the forest's vista. He was a tall man with a slightly aloof manner who seemed more mature than his seventeen years. He arrived at the same spot most evenings, yearning for the solitude and peace it brought him.

Standing proud and tall, he breathed in the refreshing water vapour which arose from the river, with its endless journey downstream to a destination he couldn't even begin to imagine. He licked the fine water vapour off his lips and savoured the slightly sweet taste as it refreshed his parched mouth.

The Shamanic Prophecy

At that time of evening with the sun going down and the forest awash with a myriad of animals calling out to each other, the villagers would be busy preparing the evening meal. But Jabuti regularly took time out to return to the soothing sights and sounds of the riverbank. With the setting sun lighting up the forest with a fiery-red glow he returned on the short walk back to the village. Negotiating a well-worn path which had taken on a slight sheen from the footfalls over the years, he took in his surroundings. Many plants grew alongside the path, which were useful to the villagers in many ways. He was still learning about them but he knew which plants could cure a fever and which ones to dress a wound.

With his musings and observations occupying his mind he soon found himself back in the village. The acrid smell of smoke coming from a fire filled his nostrils, indicating the evening meal had been prepared in his absence. A couple of dogs came bounding up to greet him and rushed around his legs, sniffing him curiously like faithful sentries. Bending down he wrestled with them as they playfully gnawed him with their canines. He loved the dogs' boundless love for anyone who gave them a little bit of affection, for not much in return it seemed to him.

The sounds of children playing filled his ears as they squealed and yelped, playing in the bare earth with nothing more than a palm frond to amuse themselves. Walking past them he ruffled their hair as they looked up at him with dirty faces and wide-eyed grins. He continued walking, smiling at his fellow tribesmen and to the women who were busying themselves preparing the evening meal. He lived as part of the Piaroa, a peace-loving tribe who lived in harmony with the forest creatures. They were a short-statured race with rounded faces and permanent smiles, in complete contrast to Jabuti's height and angular features. Their habit was to adorn themselves with necklaces and bracelets crafted from seeds and animal parts, including snake vertebrae and tapir tusks, coloured with dye from forest vegetables.

Upon arrival at the hut in which he shared with the other young men, he stooped to allow his tall frame to enter the open doorway. Immediately the forest air was replaced by a musty odour coming from many men sharing such confined quarters. He nodded his greetings and walked over to his sleeping area, which was sparsely furnished with straw matting for a bed and various personal objects tucked into a corner. That was where he spent hours whittling away on pieces of wood, recreating the animals he'd seen out hunting or whilst standing by the riverbank. He found it therapeutic to carve out life-like figures from pieces of wood which the villagers adorned their dwellings with. Occupied with his task he looked towards his two friends whom he had known his whole life.

Wanadi was a happy person with a big, wide grin which lit up his features. He had an inquisitive and playful look in his eyes which was accentuated by a large nose and a square chin. With an ever present half-smile on his lips he was always quick with a joke, in fact Jabuti was sure he had never seen him being serious in his whole life. Jabuti looked across as Wanadi's pet monkey scurried around him, which he treated with care, like a human baby, even though he had the strength of two men. He was a friend who could be relied on without question and Jabuti felt safe with him by his side.

Mapi by contrast had more of an intense personality, who had been born a natural worrier. With a rather portly countenance and wild, messy hair which seemed to stick out in every direction, he made for a bit of a comical figure. Mapi would often get upset by the teasing he got from the rest of the young men of the village, but he never let it show. What else could any man ask for? he asked himself. He had two good friends, a peaceful village to live in and food in his belly. Still he could not shake off an empty feeling deep inside his soul and which no amount of physical endeavour or contemplation could release him from. These worries seemed to shadow him from the time he opened his eyes, until the tender embrace of sleep soothed his troubled mind. Jabuti made up his mind that he would visit with the shaman to talk over his emotions that he found overwhelming. But along with that resolve came trepidation over what he might be told, or indeed find out about himself.

He liked the knowledgeable old shaman who was a peaceful man of few words, but when he did speak it was with wisdom and careful consideration. He had inquisitive, alert eyes behind his weather-beaten face, and he walked with a shuffle and the aid of a cane. No one seemed to know how old the shaman was, but to Jabuti's eyes he had always appeared old. As a child he recalled the times when he used to sit peeking through the gaps in the matting of the shaman's hut, fascinated as he treated the people who had come to seek relief for their ailments. He recalled staring in wonder as the shaman's eyes rolled back after entering into a trance from inhaling snuff, singing and chanting words which Jabuti had never heard before. He was convinced that if discovered he would be cursed for life, such was the mystery and power that the shaman held.

With a rumbling stomach his attention turned to thoughts of dinner and he suggested to Wanadi that they head off to eat. With Mapi fast asleep Wanadi took his monkey and placed it on Mapi's stomach where he promptly awoke with a start to find it looking back at him.

'Very funny Wanadi, you never get tired of that trick do you?' Mapi said, placing the monkey on the floor.

'I think we should go fishing tomorrow,' Wanadi mentioned to his friends as they walked to the communal hut where everyone ate. 'I'm getting bored of eating monkey every night.'

'I think you're beginning to look like one,' Mapi quipped.

Wanadi started imitating a monkey and chased Mapi down the path as Jabuti followed with an amused grin on his face. Climbing the steps they fell through the door giggling like little girls and were met by the surprised looks of the others gathered there.

'Three more monkeys for the pot it looks like, we will eat well tonight,' said Maru, regarding the three monkeys with a casual look as she tried to stifle a laugh.

Jabuti found that he was becoming more and more attracted to her every time they met, but he felt too bashful to speak to her properly. He immediately untangled himself, feeling embarrassed that acting like a monkey wouldn't help his chances with her much. Wanadi and Mapi nudged each other and exchanged looks, knowing all too well how fond he was of her. Every time Jabuti saw her he felt his breath catch in his throat as he gazed at her arresting beauty. He had known her since they were children, but back then he dismissed her casually as a nuisance, preferring to play with his friends instead.

But since then she had blossomed into an attractive woman and he had begun to notice bumps and curves where there were none before. Finding himself being drawn to her like a bee to honey, he slowly became intoxicated by her graceful, yet inscrutable features. He avoided looking at her, wondering what she must be thinking of him acting so stupidly. After their noisy arrival they eventually sat down for dinner, where he sat casting furtive glances her way.

The hut in which the community ate was illuminated by a blazing fire which was centrally situated with the tribe gathered around it. An all pervasive smell of smoke had permeated into the walls over the years, and the heat from the open fire added to the stifling atmosphere within. They generally cooked and ate inside due to the frequency of the daily downpours. The nightly feast could be quite varied depending on the luck and skill of the hunters, and it was supplemented with fresh produce from the communal gardens which the women tended to.

One of Jabuti's favourite foods was the peacock bass which made for delicious eating, but did not give up its succulent flesh easily. With no nets in which to catch the fish it took a patient and wily hunter, once caught though it could still catch out the unwary or uninitiated, as Wanadi knew to his cost. One day, after catching one he threw it casually into the bottom of the bongo, the name given to a dug-out canoe. As he hauled in another, the fish attached itself firmly to his foot as he helplessly hopped around the canoe on one leg almost capsizing it in the process. His friends laughed hysterically and offered him no help at all.

Relief only came when he repeatedly smashed the determined creature on the head, with the dazed animal eventually letting go.

Those kinds of stories told during the evening meal were the lifeblood of the community, and was the bond that kept them working together as a tribe. Jabuti dutifully smiled and laughed at the stories, but more often than not with a faraway look in his eyes. With their meal over the three friends walked back to their hut with Jabuti looking back occasionally trying to catch a glimpse of Maru.

'So my bashful friend, why don't you talk to her?' Wanadi asked.

'Talk to who?'

'Do you hear that Mapi, talk to who he says?' he replied, teasing him.

'I'd talk to her apart from the fact that she doesn't even notice me,' Mapi said.

'Well I'm not sure she even notices our dreamy friend over here.'

'I am right next to you two fools you know, I'm just waiting for the right moment that's all,' Jabuti replied, hoping that they would change the subject.

'Well if you don't then I will,' Wanadi joked.

'You dare do that then you're no friend of mine.'

'Do you really think I'd do that to you?'

CHAPTER TWO

They walked back to their hut in silence after Jabuti's unusual outburst, and he instantly regretted it the moment it was uttered. He tried talking to Wanadi to apologise but Wanadi offered his back as a way of response. He made up his mind that first thing the next day he would talk with the shaman before he did any more damage to his friendships. It took Jabuti a while to settle after his falling out with Wanadi, but eventually sleep embraced him in its clutches as he drifted off into a very deep slumber. In it he experienced a dream so vivid like no other he had before. He found himself at the edge of the village one morning with all the tribe gathered together with their backs turned to him, all standing in an eerie silence. There were no sounds from the dogs either that they kept as pets, which normally caused a racket at that time of the morning.

The forest was deathly quiet which was even more unsettling for Jabuti as it was usually an endless cacophony of sounds all day long. He attempted calling out to his tribe but they either couldn't hear him or they were ignoring him. He tried making his way towards them but a force seemed to pull at him from the forest, beckoning him to enter its dark and foreboding embrace. Reluctantly he took one last look at them with their backs still turned, and with a tear in his eye he turned to enter the forest; feeling himself drawn inexorably towards it. It was at that point that he felt himself being dragged backwards as the scene receded before his very eyes.

'No!' he screamed, 'I'm not ready.'

'Not ready for what?'

With the dream fading he lifted his sleep-laden eyelids to see the grinning face of Wanadi looming down upon him.

'Come on, I've been trying to wake you for an age. Must have been an interesting dream, you've been muttering and talking to yourself all morning,' Wanadi said with concern in his eyes.

'I'm sorry did I wake you?'

'I've been watching over you all morning, I've never seen you so restless.'

Jabuti instantly felt guilty for the way he had snapped at him last night, feeling warmth for the genuine concern of his friend.

'Thank you Wanadi, I shouldn't have spoken to you like that last night.'

'I don't know what you're talking about,' he replied, winking at his friend. 'Get up lazy bones, let's go and get some breakfast.'

The three friends joined the rest of the community and sat down with the shaman who had prepared the daily ritual of honey and water over which he chanted, to ward off the malevolent forces of the ancient Gods. When each member had gratefully and solemnly drunk their fill they drifted off to begin their usual chores and duties.

'Come on Jabuti, no sitting around for you,' Wanadi said.

'Just give me a moment, I'll join you later. I need to talk with the shaman.'

Wanadi and Mapi exchanged curious glances but didn't press the matter, so they bade him goodbye.

'That's fine, we'll be down by the river preparing the bongo for a day's fishing, join us when you're ready,' Wanadi told him.

Jabuti watched them amble off towards the river and took a deep breath to settle his nerves and made his way towards the shaman. He looked up from his pile of utensils which he was tying up together and looked at Jabuti in the eye.

'You've finally come to talk with me then?'

'How did you know I wanted to talk to you?'

'I've known you since you were a child Jabuti, I know when something is troubling you. I've noticed that you have been even more distracted of late, it was just a matter of time before you came to talk with me,' he replied with an encouraging smile.

'You know me better than I know myself, that's why I stayed behind to talk with you.'

'Well go ahead, I always have time for you.'

'Thank you, erm... well I don't really know where to start,' Jabuti said, gazing at the ground.

'Take your time.'

'Well, it's just that I have always had this feeling of being an outsider, and I always feel like something is missing in my life,' he began. 'I suppose I should feel grateful for the things I have but it doesn't seem enough, what's wrong with me?' he finished with a sigh.

The shaman sat in silence absorbing what Jabuti had just told him and leaned forward cupping his chin in his hands. The silence dragged on for an eternity and Jabuti started to feel decidedly uncomfortable. Finally the shaman drew in a deep breath and sat upright fixing Jabuti with a stare so piercing that he had to look away.

'Well now that you are of age I think it only right that I answer your questions. This may take some time, so I suggest you excuse yourself to your friends then come join me in my hut and I'll tell you all you need to know.'

With a feeling of trepidation Jabuti did as instructed and told his friends that he wouldn't be joining them on their fishing expedition that day. He walked away feeling bad that he had let them down and for being so secretive towards them, but they had the good grace not to pry any further. Returning to the village he wondered whether it was not too late to back out and avoid facing his fears. But he knew life would carry on the same for him, so with a heavy heart he continued walking; fearing that he might not be able to summon up the courage again.

He found himself standing hesitantly in front of the shaman's hut and taking a deep breath he walked through the open doorway. Immediately upon entering his senses were assaulted by a strong smell of burning herbs which made his head swim. He found the shaman sitting crossed-legged, enveloped in a smoky haze emanating from the smouldering incense that swirled around in a hypnotic dance. Through the smoke Jabuti's gaze was drawn towards the walls, where he noticed lucky charms and copious amounts of dried plants and the remains of desiccated animals upon the floor. Immediately he was transported back to his youth when he used to gaze in wonderment through the wall as the shaman practiced his magic.

'Jabuti, please be seated,' he invited, looking up at him. Jabuti sat down as instructed and stared at the ground not wishing to look him in the eye.

'So you have some questions for me?' the shaman asked.

'Yes,' he began, trying to find the right words, 'it seems like I spend my days as if in a trance never feeling fully engaged with my surroundings or with my friends. I feel like... I don't know...' he paused, 'it feels like I'm waiting for my life to begin and wishing for it to be tomorrow so that the next day might be better. But it never does, and I just look at everyone else living their lives happily unaware of my inner torment.

'So I find myself in front of you today wishing that I was with my friends, enjoying a day's fishing and forgetting about all this selfish nonsense,' Jabuti said, feeling irritated, talking about issues which had been plaguing him for so long.

'You know you are loved by us all Jabuti.'

'I know, but I have never had a family of my own. I have always felt like I don't belong, even though my friends' families treated me like one of their own. Maybe I'm just a bad and selfish person,' he said, feeling frustrated.

'Jabuti, stop that right now,' the shaman gently admonished him. 'You are the kindest person I know and you have suffered more than most. Now I shall tell you a secret that I and only a few others know about.'

Jabuti felt his muscles tighten and his stomach lurch as he prepared himself for what the shaman was about to tell him.

'You know all too well that your mother Pucu died during childbirth and your father died of a fever?'

He nodded in agreement.

'Well I'm afraid that what we told you about your father wasn't true, he didn't die o—'

'I don't understand. Why would you let me believe that, where is he then, why would you lie to me?' interrupted Jabuti, with a flash of anger in his eyes.

The shaman paused giving time for Jabuti to calm down and then he continued, 'You have heard tales of tall white men who have been spotted travelling in our lands?'

'Yes, but I thought these were stories told to us as children to stop us from wandering too far into the forest.'

'No they are real men Jabuti, and your father was one of them.'

'What, how could that be?'

'I know it has come as a bit of a shock, please be patient and I'll tell you all you need to know.'

'How did that happen, why did he come here, how did he find us?' Jabuti asked as the words tumbled over themselves.

'One question at a time Jabuti,' the shaman explained. 'These white men came from a world far away in vessels much bigger than our bongo, travelling for many moons to reach our lands. Their reason for doing so was to spread word of their one God in which they believed. They settled in our lands building a village many, many days' walk from here. Slowly the white men learned our language by venturing deep into the forest with just the belief of this one God to keep them safe in their travels.'

'So you met my father then, what was he like?' Jabuti asked, recovering from his initial shock.

'Well he was a serious man who had little time for the social side of village life. He spoke our language enough to be understood and we learned a lot about his lands and the reason for him coming here'

'So how did he come to find us so far away from his village?'

'Well he didn't find us, some of our hunters found him stumbling around in a state of fever deep in the forest, and they brought him back, much to the amazement of everyone. Your mother offered to nurse him back to health and that was when they first met.'

'I wish I had known her, I miss her every day,' Jabuti said with a tear in his eye.

'I know you do Jabuti.'

'What happened after he arrived?'

'Well he stayed with your mother's family even though her parents weren't happy, but your mother was headstrong and insisted upon her course of action. With her tender care over many days he slowly came to, regaining his strength and he told us of his long wanderings in the forest.'

'How long did he stay for?'

'He stayed for many moons after he became well because we would not turn our backs on one in need. We allowed him to stay on condition that he stopped talking of his God until he felt it was time to move on. He agreed eagerly as he wished to learn our language and customs, feeling that it would help him further on his travels. And so it was that your mother struck up a friendship with this mysterious man from another land.'

'What name did he go by?' Jabuti enquired.

'I think he said it was Pedro.'

'P-ed-ro,' Jabuti repeated, trying to get his tongue around the strange sounding name.

'So my mother fell in love with this man?'

'Well we were never aware of how deeply she felt about him and we did not worry because he was a religious man, thinking that he would not have any other thoughts apart from friendship towards her.'

'So what did he say when he found out?'

'He never knew Jabuti, he left before she was even showing signs. Your poor mother was heartbroken, she was a young woman with child and no partner to help share the burden.'

'I don't know what to make of all this, I feel confused,' Jabuti said as he sat deep in thought.

'It's a lot to deal with but be certain that even though your mother wasn't able to see you grow, she loved you with all her being,' he reassured him. 'But as for your father I just don't know.'

'Well that's what I have to find out then.'

'Find what out?'

'I need to find my father to talk with him and let him know who I am and learn more about him.'

'But how will you do that?'

'I will set out into the forest to find him.'

'But he has been gone for a long time Jabuti, he might have gone back to his land many moons ago.'

'Well that's a chance I'll take, I shall make my way to this village that the men of this one God built.'

'Well Jabuti that's what I have always admired about you, your head-strong nature and fearlessness,' the shaman said. 'I can see that I won't be able to talk you out of it so I give you my blessings.'

'Well I fear it might be harder than I think,' Jabuti replied, smiling at the shaman.

CHAPTER THREE

Jabuti spent the rest of the day alone, feeling the need to ponder over everything he had discovered about his past. So he walked to a part of the river where he knew he could just think and watch the fast-flowing river. Many hours must have passed, because before he knew it nightfall had descended and his mind was still in turmoil. Knowing that further contemplation would help him none he took his leave of the riverbank and returned to the village. He entered the hut silently so as not to awaken his sleeping companions and laid down on his bed, gazing through the gloom with his head resting on his hands. Before he knew it he had drifted off into a deep and dreamless sleep of the kind he hadn't enjoyed for a while.

Upon waking in the morning he felt refreshed and his mind felt somewhat clearer. With a contented smile upon his face he walked along the forest path to the river to bathe and he noticed his surroundings with a clarity he hadn't felt before. Enjoying his new sense of awareness he took a mental picture of his environment and stored it in his mind to help him on his journey. No one was forcing him to go he knew, but such was his nature that he had to leave, otherwise he would always regret having not tried. On his way back he bumped into Maru and they said hello to each other in a shy manner as Jabuti tried to avoid eye contact with her.

Jabuti decided that he had to be brave and tell her of his feelings for her before he left, 'I was wondering if you'd like to take a walk with me if you have finished your chores?' he asked with sweating hands and a beating heart.

'Well, Jabuti if you hadn't asked then I would have and that wouldn't be right now would it?' she said, looking at him in an inscrutable manner as she played with a lock of her hair.

Jabuti stood before her unsure of how to reply as he fidgeted nervously.

'It's fine Jabuti, you can breathe I'm just teasing you, that would be lovely. I'm just going to tell my mother where I'm going,' she said breezily, leaving Jabuti with a big grin on his face. He hadn't noticed meanwhile that Wanadi and Mapi had crept up on him making him jump.

'Go away you two, I'm going for a walk with Maru and I don't want to spoil it,' he said in a hushed tone.

'That's nice isn't it Mapi? We haven't seen him for over a day and when we do he tells us to go away,' Wanadi said, feigning a hurt expression.

'Looks like it's just the two of us from now on, and he hasn't even told us about his mysterious visit with the shaman yesterday,' Mapi teased.

'Stop fooling around you two, I'll tell you all about it later. That's why I'm going on this walk with Maru to tell her all about it, look shoo off both of you,' Jabuti said, pushing them gently by their shoulders.

'Fine, we'll go, but we'll be spying on you both making sure you don't get up to anything,' Wanadi said over his shoulder as they walked away laughing.

'What was all that about?' Maru asked when she returned, seeing them walk away.

'Oh nothing, ignore them,' he replied, trying to summon up some confidence. 'Shall we go for that walk then?'

'Yes that would be nice.'

Jabuti immediately felt a jolt of excitement run through his body as he tried to act all nonchalant.

'Jabuti, it's just a walk.'

'Oh yes I know.'

Their walk took them through the communal gardens which the women of the village were tending to, and they looked up at them furtively as they walked by.

'We'll be the talk of the village when we get back,' Jabuti said, looking back at them.

'I think your friends will beat them to it.'

'Well they did threaten to spy on us, but I think they were only joking as I said I had something important to tell you.'

'This sounds interesting.'

They continued walking and making small talk, enjoying the privacy of being alone, until they reached the riverbank where they both sat down.

'So what is it you want to tell me Jabuti?'

Jabuti took a deep breath then related his story of his meeting with the shaman and the news of his father. Throughout it all Maru listened intently not interrupting once, so he just continued until he finished by telling her of his decision to leave the village in search of his father.

'So I didn't want to leave before I had the chance to tell you how I feel about you…' he paused, fear coursing through his veins, 'I think I love you Maru,' he blurted out. As soon as he said it he felt foolish as he searched her eyes for some reaction, but for Jabuti the silence dragged on for an eternity.

'Please say something Maru,' he pleaded.

'Oh Jabuti…' was all she said as she ran away in tears.

He watched her run away, feeling dumbstruck and berating himself that he had ruined his only chance with her. His earlier feeling of excitement and optimism was replaced by a feeling of sadness and loneliness as he sat unable, or willing to move. He had no idea how long he had been there until he heard the voices of Wanadi and Mapi calling out to him.

'I'm here,' he called out to them.

'There he is Mapi, I told you we'd find him dreaming somewhere.'

'We were worried about you Jabuti,' Mapi said. 'We saw Maru running back looking like she was crying.'

'Yes she was,' Jabuti replied with his shoulders slumped.

'Well what were you talking about? We haven't spoken to you properly since yesterday before you spoke with the shaman,' Wanadi asked.

'I'm sorry, I haven't been a very good friend to the two of you lately have I? Let us take a slow walk back to the village then I can tell you all about it.'

The friends walked together side by side with Jabuti telling them of his meeting with the shaman and the revelation about his father and of his decision to find him. He ended by telling them of his walk with Maru, pouring out his heart to her and the feeling of embarrassment when she ran away without saying a word.

'I never knew of this Jabuti, I can't imagine how you must be feeling. You have a lot of courage my friend for making your decision to find your father, but I would rather wrestle a wild pig than tell a woman of how I was feeling about her,' Wanadi said as they laughed together, relieving some of the tension.

'A wild pig is all you'd be able to attract anyway,' Mapi joked, joining in the fun.

They continued laughing until Wanadi uttered words that Jabuti would remember and treasure until the end of his days, 'If you're brave enough to set out on this adventure then I'm coming with you.'

'Me too,' Mapi joined in without hesitation.

'I don't know what to say,' Jabuti said as tears began to form in the corner of his eyes. He knew it was no use trying to talk them out of it and he knew that he would treasure their company and friendship.

'Well that's settled then, so long as we don't have to listen to Mapi's stupid jokes,' Wanadi said, ruffling Mapi's unruly hair.

'Hey that's not fair, I make you both laugh don't I?' Mapi protested.

The next few days were busy for the friends as they made final preparations. Jabuti visited with the shaman several more times to gain more knowledge about the world outside their village. The shaman was the most widely travelled member of their society, having visited many far-flung villages due to the demand for his superior understanding of the powerful forest medicines. With the day of their departure approaching the shaman offered to meet with the friends, along with several elders to pass on any wisdom they could, in order to help them on their travels. They met one late afternoon with Jabuti and his friends all gathered around a roaring fire.

The chief of the village was also present who went by the name of Mantori who bore many scars through his years of hunting amongst the dense forest foliage. Despite his age he still possessed immense strength which was evident in his muscular torso, and with his immense stamina he could still outrun a warrior half his age. They sat discussing the dangers that the forest held, from poisonous plants, to stinging insects and jaguars. They continued talking for hours when the conversation turned to the unspoken subject of the feared cannibals which inhabited the deepest recesses of the forest.

'I would prefer to meet a half-starved jaguar than a tribe of cannibals any day,' Mantori told them.

'What can you tell us about them?' Mapi asked, wide-eyed.

'They are blood-thirsty and aggressive warriors who can hunt down their prey mercilessly. I have heard tales of these warriors running for days with minimum rest and sustenance,' he told the three friends.

'I have heard it said that they drink the blood of their victims whilst they're still alive,' Jabuti said.

'They believe they gain their strength that way, it is true Jabuti,' Yani said; one of the elders. He had a serious look about him, with sunken cheeks from two remaining teeth and a skinny under-fed look.

He knew better than anyone else how fearsome those warriors were as he had encountered them many years ago when he was just a young man. The other elders knew of his tale but he had never spoken of it since that fateful day, such was the fear that the memory evoked within him. With the fire crackling and night descending he began to tell them of his fateful encounter with the blood-thirsty warriors.

'I was on a long hunting trip which took us deep into the forest and away from the village for many days,' he began. 'We were a band of five warriors looking to find as much food as we could before we returned home. We had been hunting successfully for many days and like we had done for the past couple of nights we stopped for the night, swapping stories by the fire side. Suddenly we were startled by a sound so chilling that it set our nerves on edge.'

'What was it?' Mapi asked, entranced by his tale.

'It was the cannibals making a sound so frightening that only they know how.'

'What did you do?'

'We ran Mapi, we ran. Unfortunately in the confusion I became separated from the others and I never saw them again.'

'How did you manage to escape them?' Jabuti asked, enraptured by his tale.

'Luckily at that time I was very fit and I managed to gain some ground which gave me time to think. I could feel my skin being torn and scratched from my headlong flight through the forest, but such was the terror running through my veins I just didn't care. Several times I just wanted to sit down and give up as I felt my chest would burst, but I kept thinking of my two young children without a father to see them grow up so I kept on running for them.'

The atmosphere by the fire side was tense with an air of excitement as Yani recounted his terrible tale. His face was lit up by the glow from the fire as shadows flitted across their camp, and flames danced about as if adding their own sense of drama to his tale. He took a moment out from his story as he stared into the fire's glowing embers. Eventually he returned from his dream-like state, looking around at the faces gathered around him.

'Tell them what happened next,' Mantori gently prompted him.

Yani glanced for a moment into the inky blackness of the night as if gathering his thoughts and continued, 'In my pack I had vines for climbing trees in search of honey bees, so finding the right tree I scaled it as fast as I could and I lay hidden at the top for several days.'

'Then what happened?' Wanadi asked, drawn in by his story.

'From the top of the tree I heard them shouting and wailing. Several times I thought they had seen me but I just stayed as still as I could. I still heard them in the distance the next morning but I remained just to be sure.'

'So they didn't find you then?' Mapi asked.

Everybody laughed, as through his innocence Mapi had unexpectedly lightened the atmosphere. When the laughter died down Yani replied, 'No Mapi, luckily I never saw them again.'

'Maybe we'll be safer if we travel by bongo?' Mapi suggested, looking concerned.

'Have you forgotten what happened when we were children Mapi?' Wanadi said, reminding him of the time they borrowed the bongo without permission and were swept downstream, barely escaping with their lives.

'I know, but maybe we can avoid the rapids this time,' Mapi replied.

'Wanadi is right Mapi, you don't know what dangers the river holds downstream,' Mantori said, joining the conversation. 'Also we'll need it for fishing Mapi, I'm afraid it is too valuable a tool for you to take. And I really can't see you paddling it back upstream for days on end when you return,' he ended, trying to inject a note of kindness in his refusal.

Mapi sat in front of his fellow tribesmen looking a little crestfallen.

'I'm frightened too Mapi but if we travel by foot we'll have a better chance of remaining hidden,' Jabuti said, looking towards Mapi who was poking the fire with a stick.

The shaman and the elders took that moment as their cue to leave the three of them alone for the evening.

'If you want to stay Mapi, then I won't think any the less of you,' Jabuti said.

'Don't think you two are going without me,' he answered, looking up from the fire with a purposeful look in his eye. 'If you did then I'd never hear the end of it from Wanadi.'

Wanadi punched him playfully in the shoulder as Mapi smiled shyly like a little boy. Without talking they reached over the dying embers of the fire and linked arms in a bond of friendship and stared solemnly into each other's eyes.

CHAPTER FOUR

Jabuti's mind was still occupied with thoughts of Maru, even more so as his day of departure was looming. He avoided her by eating in his hut with Mapi and Wanadi, to save any embarrassment by bumping into her. With a continual ache in his stomach he cut a sorry figure as he ambled through the village, with his shoulders slumped and a faraway look in his eyes. I'll soon be far away, and maybe with time and distance I can begin to forget about her he thought. Of that he didn't feel so confident, but she seemed to be getting on with her life without him and so would he, he concluded. The eve of their departure arrived and the village held a large banquet in their honour. There was food of all kinds, from peacock bass, roasted tarantula, macaque, armadillo and produce from the garden, with honey as a special treat. Plenty of fermented manioc brew called sar had been prepared and everyone was encouraged to drink as much as they wished. The whole village had turned out with the three friends seated in a prominent position at the head of the festivities.

The main focus was the shaman who whirled and danced around to the beat of his rattle made from the fruit of the calabash tree, filled with magical crystals called wanali stones. The shaman's sacred instrument, brought out on special occasions was decorated with feathers from the black currasaw and macaws. Dressed in fine jewellery of a blue and white necklace and a head-dress of red and yellow feathers he made a fine spectacle. Having drunk from the hallucinogenic shavings of the capi vine he became more animated as the crowd joined in, singing and dancing. Everyone was having the most joyous time as Jabuti experienced an all-embracing sense of belonging which he had never felt before. Despite all the fun and laughter he couldn't but help notice that Maru was missing, which spoiled for him what otherwise would have been the most perfect evening. But he decided to try and forget about her and just enjoy the moment and the effort that everyone had gone to in their honour.

As Jabuti watched the festivities he was overjoyed to see Maru at the edge of the crowd beckoning him to follow her. He virtually flew to her side as she walked along the path which led to the river.

'Jabuti I'm so sorry for the way I've treated you,' she said as he joined her side.

'Oh, that's fine,' he answered, trying to catch his breath.

'No it's not,' she said. 'I want to explain, but I don't want you to say anything until I've finished.'

Nodding his agreement he let her begin.

'When you told me how you felt it came as a surprise to me as I never dreamed you thought of me in that way. But now that you are leaving I have finally realised how much I'm going to miss you. There is no excuse for me running away like that and I hope that you'll find it in your heart to forgive me,' she said, dropping her head in shame.

By then they had reached the riverbank with the full moon shining on its smooth, mirror-like surface. Jabuti took her chin in his hand and looked deeply into her eyes, kissing her passionately. He half expected her to pull away but he felt dizzy when she responded by parting her full lips and began exploring his mouth with her tongue. They stayed locked in that embrace for what seemed like a blissful eternity, with Jabuti feeling light-headed and intoxicated by the moment. Eventually they paused for breath, falling softly onto the cushioning grass, giggling as they did so. Fervently they explored each other and Jabuti heard Maru make noises of such intensity and passion that he felt he must be in a dream. Jabuti became aroused as he lay on top of her and as he stiffened he became embarrassed fearing what her response would be. Rolling off her he sighed and covered his face with his hands.

'Why have you stopped Jabuti?'

'I... I haven't done this before,' he mumbled through his hands.

'Jabuti, look at me,' she said, looking at him as she gently prised his hands away. 'Neither have I Jabuti, neither have I.'

'I don't want to do anything you don't want to,' he said, as her beautiful face looked down upon him and he found himself experiencing such a feeling of yearning, he thought his heart would burst.

Maru took his hand in hers and placed it upon her small firm breast, watching Jabuti as he stared at her in wonder. Jabuti gasped out in undisguised delight as he cupped her bosom. With the passion of the moment Jabuti took hold of her and lay her down on the lush grass, climbing on top of her as he did so. He kissed and nibbled her breasts, taking pleasure as he heard her moan and writhe underneath him. Rising up to kiss her and with her legs enveloping him he cried out in exquisite delight as he entered her. Maru responded instantly as she started kissing his neck, digging her nails into his back and holding onto him tightly as if frightened to let go of him. Arching his back with the intense passion and the pain of Maru's nails raking his back he rocked back and forth, staring into her eyes.

Jabuti longed for it to last forever but the intensity of the moment overtook his desires as he felt himself reaching a climax, gasping as he did so. He lay on top of her, panting with the exertion and felt her small firm breasts rising up and down with her laboured breaths. They remained entwined in that position, neither willing to let the blissful feeling end. Eventually Jabuti rolled over as Maru lay across his chest and he stroked and smelled the heady perfume of her long fresh auburn hair.

They awoke to the sounds of monkeys chattering and macaws squawking high up in the forest canopy. Those sounds heralded the dawning of a new day and Jabuti's departure. Feeling Maru stir he longed to lie locked in her embrace forever and dismiss such foolish thoughts of leaving her behind.

'Jabuti, I have to go before my mother gets worried,' Maru said as she awoke.

'I know you do and I have to make final plans, I am afraid of letting you go

for fear of never seeing you again.'

'Jabuti, I won't have you talking like that, you and your friends will be safe and remember that I will keep you with me in my thoughts,' she said. 'And I promise you that before I go to sleep I will remember this night we have spent together, and if you do the same then we can be together in spirit.'

'I feel so comfortable with you Maru, if I know you'll be here waiting for me then that's all I ask.'

He watched as she straightened her hair with her fingers and then bent down by the river to wash her face briskly in the cool water. Finished with her task she turned to face Jabuti, with her face glistening and the rising sun creating a glow around the outline of her body.

'This is the picture I will take with me on my journey and the one I will dream about when I go to sleep,' he told her, lying with his arms behind his head and a contented grin spread wide upon his handsome features.

'I'll see you before you go Jabuti, now I have to go before I get into trouble with my mother,' she said, blowing him a kiss as she ran down the path towards the village.

When he returned to the village people were beginning to stir, with several of them looking decidedly sick from the excesses of the night before. He entered his hut searching for his friends and found them both soundly asleep, with Wanadi's pet monkey sitting placidly on his head playing with his hair. The incongruous sight made Jabuti laugh out loud, which awoke Mapi who turned to see what the commotion was all about.

'What's all this noise about? Shut up will you my head feels like I've got a pig sitting on top of it.'

'How about a monkey?' Jabuti asked, laughing at him.

At that point Wanadi became aware of his monkey and in spite of himself he began to laugh as he took it in his arms and pretended to scold it.

'Well, this is the day of our departure,' Jabuti said as the laughter subsided.

'I'll feel more excited about it once this headache goes away, exactly how much Sar did I drink last night?' Wanadi groaned.

'I'm not sure as I was busy being sick all night,' Mapi croaked.

'I'll leave you two feeling sorry for yourselves, I've got to go and say goodbye to the shaman. Go for a swim in the river, that always makes me feel better,' Jabuti said with a smile on his face.

'I swear that man is half fish the amount of time he spends by that river. And how come he's got that big grin all over his face all of a sudden?' Wanadi said to Mapi.

Jabuti walked towards the shaman's hut receiving messages of goodwill from the villagers who were going about their daily tasks. Arriving at his destination he took a moment to gather his thoughts and entered.

'This day has finally arrived Jabuti, what thoughts are running through your head?' the shaman asked as he entered.

'Nervousness mainly, but I am blessed with the company of Wanadi and Mapi on my journey.'

'I have heard of this and you are very lucky to have two such brave and loyal friends.'

'I know, and to be honest I don't think I would have found the courage without them.'

'You would have Jabuti, I have every faith in you. Your journey would have been of a different nature, that's all.'

Jabuti found the shaman's words brought him confidence and comfort as he looked into his wise face.

'I also have to tell you that I have lain with Maru,' Jabuti mentioned, feeling shy at talking of such matters with him.

'I know all about that and I am happy for you.'

'But how do you know, it was only last night?'

'Why do you think I am the shaman?' he answered with a knowing smile.

'I hope you will be there to see us off later.'

'I wouldn't miss it Jabuti. Here, I have prepared a few lucky charms for you to carry with you on your journey.' With that he gave Jabuti a small leather sewn bag cinched tight at the top and pressed it into his palm. Inside were some lucky charms and shavings from the capi vine of which he had consumed the night before. Aside from being hallucinogenic it was believed to suppress hunger and provide extra strength when on hunting expeditions.

'It will give you the eyes of a jaguar,' the shaman said with a twinkle in his eye.

Jabuti was taken aback as the shaman arose to embrace him and held him in silence as if afraid to let go. He stood feeling helpless in his comforting grip as the warmth of his own tears ran down his cheeks. That was the start of a day of high emotions as other villagers came to wish Jabuti and his friends well on their journey. By then Jabuti had caught up with his friends, who having taken his advice had been for a swim declared that they felt thoroughly refreshed. They retired to their hut where they gathered together the tools and possessions they would need on their journey. Each pack consisted of a bow and several arrows, a blowgun with several darts laced with the curare poison, a hammock and the tools they would need for starting a fire. They also took along water carriers made from animal skins to save time stopping to drink from rivers and streams.

The three friends gathered in the communal hut for a last hearty meal with the rest of the tribe before they left on their travels. Entering together they were greeted by a chorus of cheers from the awaiting throng, and they stood overcome with emotion at the unexpected welcome. Jabuti was excited to see Maru sitting in the crowd as their eyes met with a lingering passion. That didn't go unnoticed by his friends who blew kisses at each other as they gently mocked him. Despite Jabuti's embarrassment he couldn't but help smile at his friends' antics, knowing that their good humour would keep him going when times were tough.

The shaman arose and the tribe slowly hushed as he began to speak, 'We have gathered here to say farewell to our three brave warriors who are setting out on a journey few of us would even dare to think about. Their quest is an honourable one, made even more so by the selfless and courageous actions of Wanadi and Mapi who have offered to go with Jabuti.'

Wanadi and Mapi lowered their heads, feeling slightly bashful at his words.

'Now I know that our three friends will want to be on their way well before nightfall, so I will finish by saying that you will be in our thoughts daily and we wish you well on your journey and bring yourselves back safely to us; your family,' he concluded.

After the shaman had finished it became aware to Jabuti that the tribe were looking towards him to say something, so he arose to say a few words emboldened by an encouraging smile from Maru.

Jabuti cleared his throat and began, 'I'd like to thank the shaman for his kind words and for everyone gathered here for their words of support. I'd also like to thank everyone for the celebrations of last night but I'm not so sure that Wanadi would agree.' Everybody laughed as Wanadi shifted uncomfortably. 'I have felt warmth from all of you lately and I apologise if I might have taken it for granted in recent times. I go on this journey confident and emboldened by the company of Wanadi and Mapi, two friends to whom I owe a huge debt of honour.'

With that he sat down to loud applause as they began to eat their last meal in the village for a while. They sat laughing and joking with everyone and soaked up the pleasant atmosphere, but all too soon the meal was over and it was time for them to leave. Jabuti said to his friends that he wanted to have a talk with Maru before they left and they both agreed without comment. He caught her eye as she left and they both walked together, heading in silence towards the river. When they were away from the village and sure not to be seen by anyone he took Maru's hand in his as they continued on their walk. Arriving at the river he took her in his arms and looked longingly into her warm brown eyes.

'I wanted to be alone with you one more time before I depart. I can't stay long as Wanadi and Mapi will be waiting for me, and if I did stay longer I would never want to leave your side,' he said, savouring every last moment of being alone with her.

'I will miss you Jabuti, but my heart swells with pride at your courage. There is only one man for me and I will be waiting for you, longing for your safe return,' she said, embracing him one final time as they stood not wishing to let each other go. Eventually the time came for Jabuti to return to the village, and with a steely determination he resolved to come back and spend the rest of his days with Maru.

Returning hand in hand, they couldn't take their eyes off each other and Maru laughed out loud as

Jabuti tripped over a vine, so busy was he gazing at her. Brushing himself down with his hands he managed to smile through his embarrassment. They entered the village to a farewell committee which had gathered to see the friends set off on their journey. Walking through the crowd they received warm smiles of encouragement. Eventually they made their way to the front of the gathering where they were met by Wanadi, Mapi and the shaman. There were no jokes or nudging from Jabuti's friends as it was a solemn occasion and they knew how much his new found friendship with Maru meant to him.

The shaman took Jabuti to one side to have a final word with him, 'Jabuti, I have come to look on you as my son and I am proud to have guided you throughout your life. If you find your father then I hope that his heart will swell with pride at the fine man you have turned out to be. Now go with your friends, safe in the knowledge that I will look to the spirits of the forest to guide you and keep you safe,' the shaman concluded, trying to hold back the tears that were welling up inside of him.

Jabuti turned to his two friends and bent down to gather his belongings as they turned to acknowledge the large crowd which had formed. All the women and children of the village were crying as the men attempted to comfort them. Jabuti took one last lingering look at Maru and announced to the awaiting crowd.

'We will return.'

Then the three intrepid friends turned and walked into the dark heart of the forest.

CHAPTER FIVE

Jabuti walked in silence, feeling a creeping sense of sickness at having left Maru behind; just as they were getting to know each other. The silence continued for a while until Wanadi finally spoke, 'Come on somebody, say something,' he said. 'Even one of Mapi's stupid jokes would be funny right now.'

His attempt to lighten the mood worked as they chatted between themselves and their attention turned to thoughts of food. With nightfall beginning to descend they began to look for a suitable place in which to rest up for the night. Coming across a suitable clearing they prepared a fire and swept the area with a palm frond to clear it of dead leaves, which could harbour stinging insects. With their hammocks strung up they began hunting for the monkeys they heard high up in the canopy. They had to be completely silent though as monkeys were inquisitive and skittish creatures who could scatter in an instant if alarmed.

Wanadi was armed with a blowgun as he was acknowledged to be the best of the three in its use. They had been following the sound of howler monkeys whose cry could be heard echoing through the forest from miles away. Catching sight of the troop they chose their footfalls carefully, avoiding dry leaves and twigs which would immediately announce their presence. Each one of them felt the visceral fear of the hunt, knowing that their ultimate survival depended on the death of another creature. They positioned themselves directly underneath the troop, who unsuspecting of their presence were involved in their evening chorus of howls to each other, trying to impress a potential mate and frighten off rivals.

Wanadi spotted a large male calling out, with his neck outstretched and mouth pursed, unaware of the danger which lay beneath him. Wanadi took a deep breath and sent the poison-laden dart on its silent and deathly flight into the thick fur of the unsuspecting creature. With an almost imperceptible howl of alarm it began its undignified fall to the ground, already dead by the time it hit the forest floor. Wanadi, with skill and patience succeeded in killing several more during the afternoon. Upon returning to their camp they began preparing their meal, accompanied by some manioc bread. Wanadi busied himself eviscerating the monkey whilst Mapi looked on in disgust as the thought of doing it himself made him feel quite sick. Soon the meat was roasting and crackling over an open fire and looked more tempting to Mapi.

'How far to the next village, Jabuti?' Mapi asked.

'Well the shaman mentioned that it was at least several days away and that we would expect to receive a warm welcome, for he has visited this village many times to help heal their sick.'

'That will give us plenty of time to practice our hunting skills then,' Wanadi replied.

'Yes it will, I need to practice some more with my bow and arrow and catch some fish,' Jabuti said.

'What do I do then?' Mapi asked with a glum expression.

'Come on Mapi you have skills that Wanadi and I don't possess,' Jabuti answered, sensitive to his friend's mood. 'What about the times you have sat outside a tarantula's lair with endless patience trying to catch one? Now you would never find me doing that.'

'No me neither,' Wanadi said with a look of distaste on his face.

'Well I suppose that does take a certain kind of skill,' Mapi agreed.

His friends were being kind to him though for they had never known anyone to be seriously hurt or killed by a tarantula before. In fact the children of their village were encouraged from a very early age to hunt for the spiders as it built up their skills and courage. Some children had more luck and patience than others and Mapi was one of them.

His skill came in cooking the spider, which involved searing it over a fire for several minutes and then wrapping it in banana leaves for a few more minutes which steamed the insides to rid it of parasites. Jabuti and Wanadi had enjoyed these snacks that Mapi had prepared since they were children, as others would either singe them or not cook them enough. That was a thing that Jabuti found odd about Mapi that he was squeamish about gutting a monkey, but he could quite happily skewer a live spider, watching as its legs wriggled as he poked a twig through its head. Whilst Jabuti had been reminiscing about the past their dinner had been cooked and Wanadi called over to him waking him from his reverie.

'Thinking about your girlfriend eh, Jabuti?' Wanadi teased.

'No,' he smiled, 'I was thinking back to when we were children, and here we are all these years later, still friends.'

'Well I've tried to get rid of you two but you just won't get the message,' Wanadi replied with a grin.

'Well I hope your good humour lasts my friend, for who knows how long we'll be away and what will happen,' Jabuti said.

'Well one thing I know for certain is that with me looking after you two then nothing will go wrong,' Wanadi answered.

They retired for the night soon afterwards, exhausted by their exertions. As Jabuti lay down to rest he became fully aware of the sounds and smells of the forest. Being far away from their village and all alone, he found his senses were truly heightened. Lying in the stillness of the forest he noticed the musty smell coming from the rotting vegetation that had fallen from above. He found it not an unpleasant aroma though, but rather a comforting earthy odour. Tuning into the sounds of the forest he became aware of the constant chatter of the forest's inhabitants, from the chirping and clicking of the insects, to the calls of the various species of monkeys and the sing-song of the tree frogs. With a feeling of contentment from a full belly and the company of his friends he drifted off into a deep sleep.

He awoke with a start from the calls of the howler monkeys to find Wanadi awake as well, but as usual Mapi was still sleeping right through the racket. Wanadi was just about to wake Mapi up by playing some trick on him but Jabuti said to let him sleep on. Poised just above him he reluctantly walked away with a mischievous grin on his face.

'One of these days he's going to get his own back on you,' Jabuti told him.

'I'd like to see him try,' he replied, flexing his muscles.

'Anybody who can surprise a tarantula can surprise a big old lump like you,' he said as he punched him on the biceps. 'Come on let's get the camp together and then we can wake Mapi.'

'Hey guys you should have woken me up, I could have helped you,' Mapi said some time later, wiping the sleep from his eyes.

'Well I was going to wake you with a nice slice of juicy mango, but Jabuti said you wouldn't be hungry after the meal last night,' Wanadi answered with a dead-pan face.

'What did you say that for Jabuti, you know I'm always hungry?'

There was no point in trying to correct him Jabuti thought, so he just rolled his eyes at Wanadi who chuckled away to himself. With Mapi complaining from being hungry they set off on what would be a long day of trekking through the forest.

As they were walking, they began talking about how they would approach the village as they didn't want to scare its inhabitants by just strolling in unannounced.

'I think we need to offer them a gift as a way of pleasing them,' Wanadi suggested.

'Good idea Wanadi, I think an offering of a freshly killed pig would show our generosity and skills as hunters,' Jabuti said.

'Can't we keep it for ourselves?' protested Mapi. 'I was thinking maybe a few roasted tarantulas.'

'Roasted tarantulas?' Wanadi mocked. 'Even a six year old girl can catch a tarantula.'

'Hey! You said yesterday it took a lot of skill.'

'It does Mapi, Wanadi is just teasing you as usual,' Jabuti said, trying to comfort his friend and giving Wanadi a quizzical look.

'Yes, sorry Mapi I didn't mean it to sound like that.'

Seemingly placated, Mapi protested no longer and they walked in silence with Jabuti wondering what had caused such an uncustomary outburst from Wanadi. He caught up with Wanadi who was walking ahead and decided to have a word with him out of earshot of Mapi, 'What was all that about, how come your mood has changed all of a sudden?' he asked.

'I'm sorry, I don't know what came over me.'

'Come on this isn't like you, you don't have to keep everything to yourself and keep joking all the time.'

It took a while for him to answer and Jabuti thought it best to let him respond in his own time.

'It's just that I had a disturbing dream last night,' he eventually replied. 'It was so life-like, it seemed like it really happened.'

'Come on Wanadi I've never seen you so serious, you're starting to worry me.'

'Well it really shook me, maybe it's the spirits of the forest playing tricks with my mind?'

'That's just stories we were told as kids to scare us and to stop us wandering too far into the forest. You know there are no spirits.'

'Well, whatever it was it really scared me.'

'Tell me what it was about then.'

'It started with us walking through the forest,' he began. 'It was on a day exactly like this and we were chatting away as we usually do, and then I had a feeling of being stalked by some predator. I looked around to see if I could catch a glimpse of what it was and where it was but I couldn't see anything. I looked at you and Mapi and you were both unaware of anything untoward so I just thought it was my imagination.'

'That doesn't seem too bad.'

'I haven't finished yet,' Wanadi continued, 'I still couldn't shake off this feeling even when we stopped to set up camp for the night. As we were sitting down for our evening meal there came an almighty roar coming from every direction of the forest which set my nerves on edge. Then as if from nowhere the biggest and blackest jaguar that I have ever set eyes on pounced into the middle of our camp.'

By then they had begun to slow their pace as Jabuti listened to his story. He was worried that Mapi would be aware that something was going on, but when he glanced over his shoulder he saw that he was unaware of their discussion.

'And this is the part that shocked and shamed me the most. The jaguar was prowling around in front of us all looking for the weakest prey when its hungry gaze fell upon Mapi who started to get up and run away. That set off the animal's instinct to attack which it did right in front of us as it tore poor Mapi limb from limb. I just sat there doing nothing.'

'That does sound like quite a disturbing dream but remember Wanadi, that's all it was,' Jabuti said, noticing the worry in his friend's eyes. 'Perhaps it will serve us to be more wary on our journey.'

'Yes you're probably right Jabuti, it's just that I look at Mapi and I worry that he came along to prove something to himself and us,' he said, looking back at Mapi who was walking along without a care in the world. 'If anything happens to him I wouldn't be able to live with the guilt.'

'Come on let's join him and talk no more about this.'

Wanadi immediately began play fighting with Mapi and Jabuti was relieved he had made an effort to pull himself out of his uncustomary gloom.

'What were you two talking about?' Mapi asked breathlessly afterwards.

'Nothing really, Jabuti was just saying how brave you and I are joining him on his journey,' Wanadi replied.

'Oh I see, so you were talking about me then?'

'Well we were but not in a bad way, I'm really glad you're here with us,' Wanadi answered.

'So am I,' Mapi said with a huge grin on his face.

Jabuti looked at the two of them walking together with arms over each other's shoulders and had to look away as he felt a lump in his throat.

CHAPTER SIX

The rest of the day was unadventurous as they made good progress along the forest's paths. By the end of the day Wanadi had forgotten about his dream and was back to his old self, teasing Mapi. They could tell that they were nearing a place of habitation for they were treading on a well-worn trail. Guessing that they had another day's walk ahead of them and with dusk falling they decided to set up camp again for the night. Mapi had had enough time before sunset to catch a couple of tarantulas and he set about roasting them over a roaring fire. Jabuti and Mapi had made a point of asking him to do that as they thought it would boost his confidence, and if they were honest they were looking forward to tasting its succulent flesh. They retired again for the night, happy that they had made it through another day safely and had made good headway towards their destination.

Mapi surprised them all the next morning by preparing some mango, yams and other forest fruits for their breakfast. He had also organised the camp for their departure as well, all before the other two had woken. Wanadi looked over the edge of his hammock and stared open-mouthed at the effort he had gone to.

'You see I am a man of many surprises,' Mapi said, grinning at him.

'You are indeed Mapi,' Jabuti said. 'Come on you fat lump let's eat before Mapi rolls us up with the hammocks.'

They started off on another day's walk feeling slightly nervous, yet excited at the prospect of meeting some other villagers. They had met people from outside their village before, but those visits were infrequent due to the distances involved. They had been walking for several hours when they heard a rustling coming from nearby. Slowing their pace they didn't need to tell each other to be quiet, it was just instinctive. As they neared the rustling sounds they peered through the foliage to see a large sow with a young brood close by, busy rooting through the forest debris for fresh vegetation and insects. At that moment the animals were unaware of their presence as their eyesight was poor, but they had an amazing sense of smell. Every hunter knew to approach a potential quarry from downwind to avoid the potential of spooking the animal.

At that moment they were safe from detection but as soon as they made any movement to attack then their cover would be blown as wild pigs were incredibly skittish, and could run faster than any man. They also knew that a mother who had offspring to protect could be an incredibly aggressive animal, so it had to be treated with the respect it was due. The sow did not have the visible tusks that the males had but she had incredibly sharp canines, and could charge with her head up and mouth agape, inflicting terrible wounds. The friends knew all too well about a young hunter from their village who was dismembered when he decided to tackle one on his own. With those thoughts in mind they silently withdrew in order to discuss their plan of attack. Once they had retreated to a safe distance they crouched down to confer.

'That's a big chunk of meat waiting there for us,' Wanadi said, looking forward to an exciting hunt.

'And a dangerous one as well,' Mapi replied with a note of caution.

'Yes, you're right Mapi and we mustn't forget that,' added Jabuti. 'That's why we need to make a plan.'

'We would normally have twice the amount of men we have today though,' Mapi countered.

'Yes I know, we'll just have to make do with just us three. What do you say Wanadi?' Jabuti asked.

'Well I'm up for it if you two are,' he replied.

'Right then here's the plan, we need two of us to begin the chase and another to head further up the trail, far enough to remain undetected. As the animal gets close the other one needs to break cover and chase it back towards the others, and hopefully we can corner it,' Jabuti suggested.

'I'll volunteer to be the one that waits in hiding,' Mapi said immediately.

'Are you sure Mapi?' Jabuti asked. 'That could be the most dangerous time, as the animal will be wild with fear and could charge straight at you.'

'Someone has to do it.'

'Well I'm impressed Mapi. In such a short time your bravery has humbled me,' Wanadi told him.

Jabuti and Mapi weren't sure if he was being serious or not and they waited for him to counter with a joke. When none was forthcoming they both raised their eyebrows in surprise.

'Er, thank you Wanadi.'

'That's fine, but if you tell anyone back at the village I'll deny it,' he replied with a wink.

'Right Mapi off you go but don't walk directly upwind as she'll catch your scent, you'll have to walk around until you are safe enough,' Jabuti instructed him as he nodded in agreement and watched him walk away with a confident air.

Jabuti and Wanadi both stood at the same time and headed further down the trail to better sneak up behind on the animal. They walked in silence and took position behind a large tree and waited to give Mapi enough time to get into position. Several more moments passed where they sat on their vigil and then they stood and ran towards the animal. It was initially unaware of their presence, but once it caught sight of them it squealed out an alarm to its offspring and they immediately started running away at a fast trot. Before too long the animal had opened up a small gap as Jabuti and Wanadi started to sweat through their exertions.

Jabuti and Wanadi whooped with delight at the exhilaration of the chase and they felt the muscles burn in their legs as they continued running.

'We must be getting close to where Mapi is hiding by now,' Jabuti panted.

'Well, we'll soon know,' he answered.

Just at that moment they heard Mapi shouting in the distance and soon they heard the animal's squeals and grunts coming back their way. Upon hearing that they took up position hidden from view by a large leafy plant and waited for the animal to come into view. As soon as they saw it they tensed and saw an arrow sticking out of its flank from Mapi's bow.

The animal looked crazed, grunting and squealing as it ran towards their hiding space with its mouth open and its canines showing. They weren't sure if it could see them or not, but it was definitely on a collision course with them. Swiftly they both stepped into view taking aim with their weapons, watching as they flew on a deadly flight towards the terrified animal. The projectiles hit the unsuspecting creature almost simultaneously as Wanadi's spear entered the hard hide of its flank and Jabuti's arrow embedded into the animal's skull.

The animal stopped dead in its tracks as it skidded to an undignified halt with its momentum sending it crashing through the undergrowth, landing at the feet of the two proud hunters. Just at that moment Mapi rounded the corner still yelping with the exhilaration of the chase.

'I hit it, I hit it. Did you see?' Mapi shouted out excitedly, through laboured breaths.

'Yes Mapi we saw it, I told you that between the three of us we'd be able to catch it,' Jabuti replied.

They all looked down in awe at the animal and gave thanks that they had emerged unscathed. It was at that moment that some of the piglets came into view and gathered around their mother's corpse, unafraid of the hunters' presence. They looked confused as they nudged the body with their snouts, unaware that their mother was dead. Even though they had all killed animals as was necessary to survive in the forest, their innocent display of affection moved them in a way that they had never felt before.

'What shall we do with them Jabuti?' Mapi asked, looking for some reassurance from his friends.

As the thrill of the chase subsided the sadness of the scene began to sink in. Soon they began to feel uneasy with their initial excitement of chasing the animal down to its ultimate death.

'I feel sad too Mapi,' Jabuti said, noticing the look in his friend's eyes. 'We need to chase them away I'm afraid, they'll have to take their chances in the forest. They look old enough to be weaned so they should be able to fend for themselves.'

'Do you think so?' Mapi asked.

'Yes my friend I do, and we need to avoid killing animals that have young,' Jabuti replied. 'We were a bit hasty with this kill, we need to be more respectful in the way we use the abundance the forest provides.'

With that they shooed the animals away until they were alone with their kill.

'You know this is a big animal,' Wanadi pointed out. 'How are we going to carry it between us all the way to the village?'

'Good point Wanadi, that's another reason why we were too hasty. Looks like you will taste some of its meat after all Mapi.'

'I don't know whether I can after what I have just seen.'

'Come on Mapi, if you think like that then you'd never eat anything. After putting up such a brave fight the least we can do is put its meat to good use. Wanadi and I will prepare it and I'm sure once you smell it cooking you'll change your mind,' Jabuti said, placing a comforting hand on his friend's shoulder.

'Yes perhaps you're right.'

'You prepare a camp for the night and we'll get on with our work here,' Jabuti said.

'I'm glad to see that Mapi hasn't changed completely,' Wanadi said, when he was out of earshot.

'Me too, I like his new found confidence but his sensitivity is a good thing as it will stop us doing anything rash or foolhardy.'

Wanadi and Jabuti busied themselves with the carcass, making sure to keep a large part aside as a gift for the village they were heading towards. They kept one side of the flank for themselves and the remainder aside, including the hind quarters which were the tastiest and tender parts of the animal. Nothing went to waste in the forest and every part of the animal was consumed including the head, which made a tasty broth. They wrapped up the parts they weren't using in large palm leaves which would keep it fresh and keep insects away.

Mapi soon returned, proud to inform them that he had set up a camp and had already lit a fire and pronounced that he was starving and couldn't wait to get the pig roasting! Jabuti and Wanadi followed him with smiles upon their faces and sat around the blazing fire and chatted amongst themselves.

'So when do you think we'll reach this village Jabuti?' Mapi asked with his mouth full.

'I thought we might have reached it tonight as the trail we've been following all day looks well-trodden,' he answered. 'I think by tomorrow we should be there, if not then it's pig for you every night.'

'I don't have a problem with that,' he said, eyeing up the next morsel.

'I'm not running and sweating through the forest chasing after a pig so Mapi can eat it all,' Wanadi said, teasing him again.

'Hey! I can't help it if I've worked up an appetite hunting down that pig, it was a long walk you know,' he protested. 'And I was all on my own.'

'It's just as well Jabuti and I were there to help you catch it then wasn't it?' Wanadi continued, enjoying getting a reaction from his friend.

'Well I have to say you did help a bit, I think my arrow fatally wounded it and it was only a matter of time before I caught up with it and finished it off,' he said. 'Go on help yourself Wanadi, you've earned some,' he said, pointing to the remainder of the carcass roasting over the fire.

'You're a…' Wanadi started to say but stopped himself when he looked over at his friend and realised that he had been played at his own game. 'Yes fine, you got me I must admit,' he said, holding his hands up with a smile.

'Oink, oink!' Mapi said, winking at his friend.

They retired soon afterwards with glad hearts and full bellies. Jabuti lay rocking in his hammock, reflecting about their journey so far and suddenly the realisation of the enormous task he had set himself and his friends hit him. Immediately a whole barrage of doubts entered his mind uninvited. What if I never get to find my father, what if he doesn't want to talk to me, what if he doesn't like me? he thought in desperation. With the teasing embrace of sleep eluding him he sat up in his hammock and swung his legs over the side, glancing at his friends who were still sound asleep and gently snoring.

An overwhelming feeling of loneliness immediately swept over him as he sat looking at them sleeping peacefully. He hopped off his hammock and took another look at them with the hope that one of them might wake up. Seeing that they were still asleep he sighed and started off on what he promised himself would be just a short walk. He proceeded to walk along the well-worn path that they had been following all day. He didn't know how long he had been walking when all of a sudden he became overwhelmed by a barrage of emotions which stopped him dead in his tracks. Standing all alone he felt a river of tears well up inside of him, and before long his body was assailed by uncontrollable sobbing coming from deep within him. What's happening to me? he thought.

Jabuti felt a lifetime of self-doubt and loneliness building up within him, reaching a crescendo which threatened to engulf him with its sheer intensity. After what seemed like an eternity the tears subsided as he curled up on the ground and he brought his knees to his chest and hugged and rocked himself, trying vainly to soothe his troubled mind. Falling asleep in that position he awoke some time later to the sensation that something was crawling up his arm and he brushed it off without thinking. He immediately screamed out as the creature bit him and he hugged his arm to his chest crying out in pain.

Little did he know that he had been bitten by the wandering spider which was the most venomous spider in the forest. What he did know was that something wasn't right as he had trouble breathing and he began to lose muscle control rapidly. He feared that if he didn't make it back to the camp somehow he might well die alone and never realise his destiny. With incredible effort and with a searing pain running through his veins he managed to get to his knees and fought the dizziness to eventually stand up. He lurched forward as the path became blurred and with his vision worsening he had to trust in his instincts that he was heading the right way.

He tried calling out to alert his friends but his throat had become restricted and he began to panic with laboured breaths. Suffering deep cuts and grazes he stumbled blindly through the undergrowth. Fortunately the noise he made eventually saved his life as the commotion had aroused virtually every creature in the forest. The screeching and squawking also awoke Wanadi and Mapi with a start. Noticing that

Jabuti's hammock was empty they sensed that their friend was in trouble and in need of their assistance. Immediately alert after their slumbers they ran towards where the sounds were coming from, calling out Jabuti's name all the while.

'He's not answering Wanadi, maybe we should go back and get some weapons, what if he's been attacked?' Mapi said.

'I don't think so Mapi, I think he's wandered off for some reason and got into difficulties,' Wanadi answered. 'Otherwise we would all have been attacked whilst we were sleeping.'

'So how do we find him then?'

'We just follow this noise.'

They soon heard the commotion of crashing undergrowth to see Jabuti stumbling into their vision with a wild and frightened look in his eyes as he fell unconscious into their arms.

CHAPTER SEVEN

'You look just like your father,' came a voice that Jabuti did not recognise as he tried vainly to open his eyes. Was he dead, who did the voice belong to, was it the voice of the white men's God? he wondered in his half-dreaming state. He was sure he could hear children playing nearby, but no sooner had those sounds filled his head than he drifted into unconsciousness again. Some time later and with a pounding head he eventually came round and he propped himself up wearily on his elbows. He found he was lying in a small hut constructed in the manner of his home village and immediately he thought that he was back in his home village. With the prospect of seeing Maru again he found his heart thumping and a jolt of electricity ran through his body. Holding onto the wooden frame of the hut he pulled himself up to stand but regretted it the second he crashed onto the floor in a heap.

He awoke to find his head being cradled as water was being gently poured into his parched mouth.

'Hello my friend,' came a voice he instantly recognised. 'What were you doing? You have to take it easy.'

'Wanadi?' he managed to croak through dry and cracked lips.

'Hello Jabuti,' he heard Mapi say.

'Mapi, are we back home, how long have I been here?'

'No Jabuti we're not home.'

Jabuti felt a great sadness and anger at not being able to see his beloved Maru, and he slumped back onto the ground.

'We're at the village we were heading to, you've been lying here for three days,' Mapi told him.

'Three days?!'

'You were very ill,' Wanadi said. 'You were bitten by a wandering spider, the shaman of this village has been treating you. He said you were very lucky to survive as he has seen men paralysed by its poison before.'

'His must be the voice I heard.'

'What did he say to you?' Wanadi enquired.

'He said I look just like my father.'

'Yes that's what he has been saying ever since we arrived,' he told Jabuti. 'We caused quite a commotion barging into the village in the early hours of the morning, shouting for help. Once they got over the shock of our sudden arrival and with you being so ill they have been incredibly kind and generous.'

'The shaman keeps coming in to look at you,' Mapi said. 'He keeps saying it's like meeting your father all over again.'

'So he knew my father?' Jabuti asked with excitement lighting up his features.

'Yes, and they have said we can stay for as long as it takes for you to become well again,' Wanadi informed him. 'He told us to fetch him when you awoke so that he could come speak with you.'

'Yes I would like to meet him and offer my thanks.'

With that they left him to go in search of the shaman.

Lying back down he immediately felt better knowing that his two friends were by his side once again, but his happiness was tinged with sadness knowing that he would not be seeing Maru. It was good that they had not returned home somehow he thought, because he knew he would never have been strong enough to leave her side again. Staring up at the ceiling he became lost in thoughts of her, with their last encounter together playing through his mind as if it were yesterday. He imagined a scene where they were walking by the river hand in hand, having returned safely from his travels and living together as man and wife.

He was broken out of his daydreaming though as a big bear of a man entered the hut and introduced himself as Rapau, the shaman. With a warm smile, gleaming white teeth and arms that looked like they could break a log in two, Jabuti felt instantly at ease. He was a little surprised to see a shaman so young and strong as he was the exact opposite of their wise old shaman. But when he spoke with a gentle and calming voice it became clear to Jabuti that he could imagine people coming to see him, seeking his advice.

'It's incredible,' he said. 'It's as if your father was sitting before me all those years ago.'

'So you knew my father well?' Jabuti asked him.

'Not well, but Maoira introduced me to him whilst he was staying in your village.'

'Who is Maoira?'

'The shaman from your village, have you never sought to ask his name?' he asked with a look of surprise on his face.

'Well, no not really. I've always known him as the shaman since I was a child. It seemed disrespectful to me to address him by his first name,' Jabuti told him. 'Everyone just calls him shaman. What were you doing in our village?'

'Maoira asked me to help treat your father as he had never seen an illness like his before. I hear you and your faithful friends are on a journey to find him?'

'Yes, as soon as the shaman told me about him I knew I had to find him.'

'Well I think you are all very brave,' Rapau told him. 'Now rest up and I'll leave you in peace. I hope you can join us as our guests for dinner this evening. There are plenty of people who want to meet you and your friends. It's not often that we get visitors.'

'But I have more questions,' Jabuti said, sitting up, reluctant for the conversation to end.

'Jabuti, there is plenty of time,' he said, resting his huge hand on his shoulder. 'You need to get your strength up.'

Finding himself alone again Jabuti tried to get to his feet, but he still felt a bit unsteady. Noticing that a large bowl of water had been placed on a wooden stand he splashed some over his face then poured the rest over his head, enjoying the invigorating feeling it provided. Rubbing the excess water from his body, he noticed that there was some kind of poultice wrapped in vine leaves on his left arm. Touching it gently he found that it didn't hurt but it gave off rather a strange kind of comforting and throbbing sensation.

Standing by the doorway and letting himself dry off, he regarded the comings and goings on of his new environment. Even though he was not familiar with the new village and its inhabitants, life seemed pretty much the same as it was in his home village. There were women sitting in the shade of a large tree preparing manioc bread, children running around laughing and playing and the occasional sound of dogs barking. As he regarded his new surroundings he noticed his friends walking across the open ground towards him with some fruit, and for the first time since awakening he realised that he was starving.

'The patient has recovered Mapi,' Wanadi said with a big foolish grin.

'How are you feeling?' Mapi asked.

'I'm feeling a lot better thanks to you two, I haven't had the chance to ask you what happened in the forest after I got bitten. I can't remember a thing after that.'

'You were in a bad way,' Mapi began. 'We awoke to the sounds of the whole forest coming alive and that's when we noticed that you weren't in your hammock. So we followed the sounds to find you crashing through the undergrowth. That's when Wanadi hel—'

'Mapi, we don't need to talk about that now,' Wanadi interrupted him, looking slightly embarrassed 'He's safe now and that's all that matters.'

'We have no secrets between us Wanadi, he needs to know,' Mapi said. ' I must admit that I panicked a little when I saw you in such a state, but Wanadi remained calm. He noticed a swelling on your arm, so he cut the skin and sucked the poison out. Rapau said that that was what saved your life.'

'Come on, any one of you would have done the same. Anyway it was both of us who helped carry you here,' Wanadi replied and shifted uncomfortably on his feet.

'Well, I appreciate it,' Jabuti said. 'If you hadn't have found me then I could have died.'

Silence then ensued as they didn't know what else to say to each other as Jabuti busied himself fiddling with his arm bandage.

'Rapau said not to touch it or your arm will fall off,' Wanadi said, breaking the silence as they burst out laughing.

They spent the rest of the afternoon walking around the village as Wanadi and Mapi introduced Jabuti to the inhabitants. They were still talking with the men of the village when dusk fell and they were invited as guests of honour for the evening meal. The occasion found them sitting with Rapau and several other villagers who listened eagerly as they spoke of Jabuti's search for his father.

'So where will you go once you leave here?' Rapau enquired of the three friends.

'We're just going to head downstream to the place where the white men come from,' Jabuti said.

'That is where the shaman…Maoira, sorry. That is where he said the white men built their village after crossing the water that has no end.'

'Yes, that's what I heard from your father as well,' Rapau answered.

'What do you think my chances of finding him are?' Jabuti asked, looking for reassurance.

'You have to try is all I can say to you, we did get another white man enter our village a long time after your father had left and he stayed with us for a few days,' Rapau continued.

'What did he say, did he talk of my father, is he still there?' Jabuti asked of him in quick-fire succession.

'Well he did talk of him but I don't know if he is still in our lands.'

Wanadi and Mapi exchanged expectant glances with Jabuti, glad for him and themselves that they had some more recent news. Rapau noticed their expectant faces and so without any more prompting he continued with his tale.

'I told this man that I had helped heal your father and I had got to know him quite well. He stayed with us for several days and we learnt more about his lands and their customs. He told us that your father had returned to their village after a long time of travelling, complaining of feeling unwell.'

'Is he dead?' Jabuti asked with a feeling of dread.

'No, Jabuti he's not dead. Well he was still alive last I heard from this white man, but he said that his illness would return from time to time which would leave him very weak. The elders of his village told him to go back to his land to recover but he refused saying that his work was more important than his health. I admire his courage Jabuti even though what he did with your mother was not honourable.'

'He has an inner strength Jabuti, just like you,' Wanadi interjected.

Jabuti smiled at his compliment then asked of Rapau, 'How long ago was it that this man came to stay?'

'It must have been when you were embarking on manhood.'

'He might still be there Jabuti, that wasn't long ago at all,' Mapi said, full of hope. 'If he was able to overcome his fever, and if he really was a true believer in his God then we might still find him.'

'Well, let us all hope so Mapi,' Jabuti said.

'I think this calls for a celebration with some Sar,' Rapau told them, and asked one of the teenage boys sitting nearby to go fetch some.

'Oh no, keep that stuff away from me!' Wanadi said, pulling a face.

The Sar duly arrived and despite himself Wanadi couldn't help but have a drop or two. Before too long Rapau and the rest of the village were happily drinking, eating and laughing with their new found friends.

CHAPTER EIGHT

Rapau breezily entered their hut the next day bidding them a good morning, seemingly unaffected by the previous night's festivities.

'Look at you three, you look as sick as dogs,' he said laughing. 'Wanadi, I've never seen anyone drink as much as you.'

'Well I won't be drinking any more ever again,' he managed to say through dry lips.

'That's what you said last time,' Mapi reminded him.

'What are you, my mother?' Wanadi replied.

'If I was I couldn't have given birth to one as ugly as you.'

'I think you two are still drunk, Rapau have you got anything to shut these two up?' Jabuti groaned.

'A good breakfast and a day out hunting should do it,' he replied. 'We heard that you had killed a pig to give to us but lost it after Jabuti was bitten. So we'd like to return the favour, but you should remain here Jabuti and build your strength up,' he said.

Rapau, Wanadi and Mapi gathered with weapons assembled after eating breakfast and Jabuti was there to see them leave.

'We expect you to have baked us some manioc bread for our return,' Wanadi said, alluding to the fact that it was only women who engaged in that task.

'You heard Rapau, I have to take it easy,' Jabuti teased back.

Jabuti chuckled, watching the hunting party leave with Wanadi and Mapi trailing behind with sick faces. He decided that in their absence he would make some wood carvings to thank Rapau and his fellow villagers for their generosity. The morning passed quickly as Wanadi impressed Rapau with his skill in using a blowgun. Reasonably confident in their skills as hunters he called a halt for lunch, which they carried in leather pouches strung over their shoulders. It was a simple meal of dried monkey meat with fruit from the moriche palm tree which was in season.

'So how exactly are you going to find Jabuti's father then?' he asked of the two friends after they had eaten.

'Well, we are going to continue downstream to where the water has no end,' Mapi replied.

'Yes I know that already but I hoped you had more of a plan, that's all' Rapau replied with a furrowed brow.

'What troubles you?' Wanadi asked of him.

'I admire your bravery in setting off on this adventure,' he said. 'But somehow I can't help but worry that you could be heading for danger.'

'How so?' Wanadi enquired.

'Have you not heard of the cannibals who inhabit the region downstream?' he asked.

'Well yes, one of our elders told us of a terrible encounter with them and he barely escaped with his life,' Wanadi answered.

'And that tale does not scare you?'

'Yes it does,' Mapi replied. 'But we knew that Jabuti was determined to set forth on his journey and we promised to come along and help him.'

'And you are willing to risk your lives following him into lands you have never even seen; unsure of where to go?'

'Rapau, we appreciate your generosity in helping us but I feel uncomfortable with you questioning us so,' Wanadi said, feeling slightly irritated.

'Wanadi!'

'It's fine Mapi I was just testing your resolve and loyalty. But please be careful, you will be heading into areas none of us have ever seen before, but I know Jabuti will be safe with you two by his side,' he said with a huge grin as he leaned forwards and slapped them both on their shoulders.

Despite himself Wanadi smiled broadly, feeling like a child who'd just received a compliment from his father.

'So tell me more about Jabuti and your friendship with him,' Rapau asked.

They looked at each other and Mapi took it upon himself to tell Rapau, 'Jabuti has always been a bit different from the rest of us, he often sets out on long walks by himself. Most times he can be found by the river gazing across its expanse as if lost in a dream. But when we are together he is a funny and loyal friend, but for some reason known only to himself he keeps a certain part of himself secret even to us; his closest friends,' Mapi stopped, feeling slightly conscious of talking about Jabuti behind his back, but after an encouraging smile from Wanadi he continued.

'So when he told us of his conversations with our shaman I knew straight away that I would help him. If he can find his father and finally find some peace, then I will him follow wherever he wishes. Somehow I feel that as long as we are together then we'll be safe.'

Rapau smiled warmly when he had finished and spoke to both of them, 'That is something that Jabuti should be proud of indeed, to have the two of you for company. I have only known you for a short time but I feel warmth for you all. Your friendship must be very strong that you would risk your lives for him. I just know in my heart that you will be safe and you will find what you are looking for.'

'Thank you Rapau,' Wanadi replied. 'I think what happened to Jabuti has made us more cautious and we will be careful, I promise.'

'Good my friends, let us not talk any more of this.' With that he arose and embraced them in a hug so fierce that it almost took their breath away.

They continued hunting throughout the afternoon and returned to the village in good humour as dusk was falling. Jabuti met them on their arrival and enquired about their day.

'Nothing to tell really,' Wanadi said to him. 'We were just talking about tasting the bread you've baked for us.'

Rapau smiled warmly at the three friends as they continued teasing each other. He knew that with Jabuti's strength returning they would be on their way soon and with that thought he felt a tinge of sadness. What will happen to them, will Jabuti ever find the peace he seeks? he wondered.

They stayed for two more days as Rapau fussed over them making sure that they had hunting tools, fresh supplies and hammocks. The friends felt embarrassed with his kind offer and said that they would try to retrace their steps to recover their equipment. Rapau wouldn't hear of it though and insisted that they take them as parting gifts.

A breaking dawn found the three friends saying goodbye once more, to new found friends. Rapau felt genuinely sad and showed his emotions as only he knew how, by giving the three friends a warm embrace as Wanadi and Mapi braced themselves for what was coming. Lastly he hugged Jabuti, who was taken by surprise at his strength, but like his two friends he found the emotions generated within him were warm and powerful. With that they entered the forest and paused to turn around and wave to Rapau who stood with a look of sadness in his eyes.

CHAPTER NINE

'Next time don't go walking off on your own,' Wanadi said after a period of silence and with a playful glint in his eye.

'Yes, I'm sorry about that, I put us all in danger,' Jabuti replied, looking away in shame.

'Well, I didn't want to ask,' Wanadi began, not wishing to pry, 'but why exactly did you walk away on your own?'

Jabuti took several moments before answering and began, 'I don't know really, I couldn't get to sleep with thoughts racing around in my mind. So I was lying in my hammock thinking about my father and worrying if he would want to see me and what he would think of me. I suddenly felt really lonely and I looked across, hoping to find one of you awake so that I could talk to you.'

'You should know by now that you could have woken one of us up Jabuti,' Mapi said.

'Thank you Mapi, I didn't want to bother you though, so I thought a short walk would help to clear my mind. I began walking and after a while I just erm, well I …' Jabuti said falteringly, with tears beginning to form in the corners of his eyes.

'Jabuti, you don't have to continue. But if you want to, remember you are among friends,' Wanadi told him.

'Well, I don't really know what happened,' Jabuti began again, 'I suppose it was all these years of feeling different, searching for something I just can't grasp. It just seemed to catch up with me and after walking for a while I just sank to my knees, and then I…' Without saying a word Wanadi took him in his arms and embraced him.

'Listen, if I wanted a girlfriend I would have gone out with Mapi,' Wanadi said after a while with perfect timing, as he gently pushed Jabuti away.

'As if I'd go out with a big lump like you,' Mapi said, feigning being hurt.

'Oh yes, something you want to tell us eh, Mapi?'

'You're the one who said he wanted a girlfriend.'

'Ooh I love it when you get angry, you look really pretty,' Wanadi said in a high-pitched voice as he blew kisses at him and pinched his behind

'Get off, there's something wrong with you I swear,' Mapi said, smirking.

Many days passed without incident and Jabuti felt that with each foot forward he was closer to achieving his goal. He found it a bittersweet feeling though, as the further he trekked away from their village his memories of being with Maru and standing by the river became more distant. What if I'm away for months and her feelings wane, or even worse; what if she falls for someone else? he thought. He was brought out of his gloom though by a smell of smoke which was drifting towards them. They were cautious as they had been on their own for almost a week after leaving the company of Rapau, and his words were still fresh in their minds about the ever present danger of cannibals. Gathering together they conferred in hushed tones.

'What do you think Jabuti, shall we go and investigate?' Wanadi asked.

'Yes, I think we should have a look. But we need to be careful because we don't know who they could be,' Jabuti answered.

'Have you noticed that there are no paths around here,' Mapi observed.

'And?' Wanadi asked.

'A-n-d,' Mapi replied, 'that means that we're not near any villages, so whoever it is must be a long way away from home as well. So it must either be a hunting party, or…' he trailed off, letting his words hanging in the air.

'You're right Mapi, well spotted,' Wanadi replied. 'We've allowed ourselves to become lazy, I must admit that I hadn't noticed that.'

'That means we need to be extra careful then,' Jabuti said. 'We need to tread softly, and I think only one of us should go and investigate.'

'I'll go,' Wanadi offered.

'Thanks Wanadi but you're such a big lump that there's more chance of you being seen in the daylight,' Jabuti said with a smile.

Wanadi looked crestfallen as he was the kind of person to volunteer for anything despite the danger, but he knew it made sense so he didn't pursue the matter.

'I'll go, I brought you along on this journey so I want to check it out.'

'Be careful Jabuti, at the first sight of danger then come right back and we can find another way forward,' Wanadi warned him.

With that Jabuti nodded and set off to where the smoke was drifting from. He walked with eyes fixed alternately to the forest floor and ahead of him for anything that might give away his presence. Silently he negotiated his way through the tangled forest floor, avoiding dry leaves and anything that he could trip over. With sweat forming on his brow and obscuring his vision he had to stop every few minutes to wipe it from his eyes. With his senses heightened for any strange noise or movement, Jabuti could feel the beating of his heart pounding in his ears as he inched his way closer.

As he followed the smell he made out voices, but it was in a tongue that he had never heard before. Alarmed, he stopped suddenly and crouched down to give himself time in which to think. Should I turn back and find another way forward, or should I carry on and see who these strange voices belong to? he wondered. He decided to continue however, feeling drawn towards the voices like a moth to a flame.

He felt that with every step he made would give away his presence, and every sound he made however small became magnified in his head. Sensing that he was within touching distance he lowered himself to his belly and began to shuffle his way closer. Ever present in his mind was the danger of stinging insects of the kind he had just encountered, but that was the chance he had to take if he was to remain undiscovered.

As he approached he saw the figures of three men sitting by a fire. Silently and slowly he parted a large leaf that obscured his field of vision and what he saw made him gasp. White men!

Letting the leaf fall back into place he gathered his thoughts. He decided to return to his friends to discuss the importance of what he had just seen. Shuffling backwards on his elbows and knees he kept a wary eye on them. With his attention focused to the front he failed to pay attention to his retreat and the fact that a twig had become entwined in his loincloth. Withdrawing further it snapped as it reached its breaking point and the sound in the stillness magnified in Jabuti's head like a tree crashing to the ground. Inwardly groaning he lay hugging the ground for comfort, hoping to remain undiscovered.

'*Qué pasa*?' one of them asked.

'*No sé,*' one of the others said.

Jabuti listened to the white men speaking in their strange language, aware nonetheless that they were reacting to the sound they had just heard. To Jabuti's horror he saw one of the men dispatched to investigate. Jabuti was torn between lying still, hoping to remain undiscovered or to make good his escape. Deciding on the latter he slowly rose to a crouched position to flee.

'*Mira, mira aquí*!' the man cried out as the others looked to where he pointed, where they saw Jabuti running away.

'Friend, come,' one of the men called out in Jabuti's own language and he immediately stopped dead in his tracks.

Shocked by what he heard and unable to help himself he turned around slowly to face the three men, who stood in the distance beckoning him to come forth with arm gestures.

'Who are you?' Jabuti asked, shocked by how loud his voice sounded after his silent vigil.

'Friends, friends-come,' one of the men said with a smile upon his face. At that point he elbowed his two companions who responded with fixed grins upon their faces.

Jabuti stood rooted to the ground still amazed at his encounter. The shaman and Rapau had both told him how there were white men like them who had the skill to speak their language, but Jabuti hadn't expected to meet any so soon. Rapau had said that their village was many, many days' walk away and Jabuti knew that they were nowhere near as yet.

He stood in front of them feeling uneasy as he weighed up his options. He could run away but that could lead them straight to his friends. If he did run away he would always regret not knowing if they could help him find his father. As those thoughts ran through his mind he eyed up the man who seemed to be their leader. He was a tall man with a muscular build like Wanadi and with a confident look on his handsome face. He had a dirty and straggly beard which was interrupted by an angry looking scar which ran down the right side of his face and down to his chin.

He held what looked like a weapon to Jabuti with a wooden grip and a fanciful long snout attached to it. Jabuti couldn't take his eyes off the beautifully sculpted object as it glistened in the sun's rays. He also carried two smaller weapons that were strapped around his waist, giving him a slightly menacing aura. Jabuti proceeded towards them with caution regarding the other two as he did so.

The man who stood to the right of the tall man was as fat as he was tall, with sweat soaking his clothes fully. Jabuti wondered how anybody of that size could survive the heat of the jungle, having never seen anyone so large before.

As he tore his eyes away he regarded the other man with caution, as there was something in his eyes and the way that he was smiling which made Jabuti distrustful of him. He was nearly as tall as the one with the weapons but the exact opposite of the fat man, with skin stretched over bone and a constant tic underneath his left eye. Jabuti approached them cautiously and the tall muscular man leant towards him with his hand outstretched, which made Jabuti recoil instantly. With that the skinny man stepped forward in an aggressive manner.

'*Ya basta idiota*!' the taller man barked at him.

He stepped back into place instantly, reacting like a scolded dog.

'Sorry, no afraid. Sit, sit,' the leader said, pointing to the fire they had made.

'Drink, drink?' he asked eagerly, pointing to something steaming in a container on the fire.

'No, thank you,' Jabuti politely declined. 'How have you learned our language?'

'Slow, please,' he said.

Jabuti repeated his question more slowly.

'Aah!' he exclaimed. 'We learn many years here, tribes our friends.'

'You come to talk of your one God?' Jabuti asked.

'God? yes, yes,' he said. 'I Diego,' he said with his hand to his chest, 'he Miguel and he Alonso,' indicating the skinny one and the fat man in turn.

'I am Jabuti,' he replied. 'You come from the village where the water never ends?'

'By water, yes,' he answered, not understanding fully as the other two remained silent. Maybe they hadn't learnt his language or maybe their leader did all the talking Jabuti thought.

'Where you from?' Diego asked.

'A village far away, upriver.'

He seemed to understand and asked, 'What you do here?'

'Hunting,' Jabuti said, not wanting to give away too much.

'Alone?'

Feeling a little uneasy in their presence he told them that he was indeed alone as he didn't want to involve Wanadi and Mapi as yet.

'Dangerous, no?' Diego asked with a menacing stare which made Jabuti feel uncomfortable.

'No.'

'No problem,' he said holding his hands up in a placatory gesture. 'You come with us, talk of God yes?'

'I can't, I have to go,' Jabuti said as he sensed a shift in the atmosphere.

'No come, come. You far from home, you come rest,' Diego said and he stood up suddenly.

Jabuti instantly recoiled and tried calling out to his friends as he scrambled to his knees, but before he knew it he felt his arms pinned behind his back and a gag was violently stuffed into his mouth. He looked across to Diego who stood grinning with his hands on his hips and the fat one staring uncomfortably at the ground.

What was going on? he thought in panic. One moment he was walking happily with his friends nearing their destination, and the next his whole world had changed in a sudden and dreadful instant.

CHAPTER TEN

'Jabuti has been gone for some time Wanadi.'

'I know Mapi, we'll give him a little longer. We don't need to worry just yet, he did tell us just to sit still,' he said, giving Mapi a reassuring smile.

Several long moments passed without a sign of Jabuti returning and by then Wanadi had become a little concerned.

'Let's go and have a look Mapi,' he decided.

With their senses heightened they were alert to every sound as they made their way over gnarled tree roots, twisted vines and creepers. They lowered themselves to a crouching position as the pungent smell of the fire grew stronger. Pulling broad leaves apart to clear their vision they slowly crept into the makeshift camp to find the fire smouldering away on its own.

'Where is he Wanadi?'

'I don't know Mapi,' he answered, looking around the camp bewildered. 'He can't have gone far though.'

'But why would he have left without telling us?'

'He didn't have a choice Mapi,' he said, pointing to a patch of flattened foliage and broken branches, indicating signs of a furious struggle.

'What do we do?' Mapi asked.

'We follow, Mapi. That's what we do.'

'And then what?'

'Mapi, I don't know,' Wanadi replied slightly exasperated. 'We don't know who's got him. But I do know it's no local tribe, they know nothing of forest craft' he said as he crouched down to inspect the messy trail they had left.

'Come on,' he called out as he set off at a trot in pursuit of his friend.

Meanwhile Jabuti was sweating and finding it hard to breathe, as they had placed a hood over his head which made him panic in its claustrophobic envelope. He heard muffled shouts coming his way as they poked and prodded him continuously. Several times he tripped over and they pulled him up roughly and he felt his shoulders almost pop out of their sockets. Where are they taking me, if they are not men of God, then who are they? he thought. With fear starting to grip him he struggled against his ties and then felt a crashing blow to the back of his skull. He was sent tumbling to the forest floor with the force, and he felt the bitter tang of bile rise up the back of his throat. He forced it back down though, fearing he would choke on it with the gag in place. Afraid of another beating he tried to curl up into a ball and he heard them arguing. After lying on the floor for some time he found himself being lifted up, but with more care.

'No fight, friend,' he heard being whispered into his ear.

After several hours of walking, Jabuti became aware of a sickly-sweet odour permeating the heavy cloth of the hood. He tried hard to breathe through his mouth as the cloying smell permeated his nostrils, making him retch. Unconcerned for his comfort they continued pushing him roughly in his back as he stumbled blindly forwards and he became aware of ululating voices ringing out to the tree tops, setting his nerves on edge as they got closer. With beating drums and the deep timbre of voices, Jabuti felt his chest vibrate with its intensity. Suddenly he became aware of people reaching out to stroke and caress him and he recoiled instantly at their touch as they jabbered excitedly in a language that was alien to him. At that moment Jabuti had never felt so alone or scared in his whole life.

As he was pushed through the agitated crowd he felt the intense heat of a fire as they came to a halt. Suddenly his hood was snatched away and he screamed out in horror when he saw a monstrous face looking down upon him. With wild, staring eyes and a huge lolling tongue hanging down its chin, Jabuti flinched at the sight of a tall wooden carving looming menacingly above him. Looking around he became aware of terrifying warriors who were closing in all around him. He stared in horror at their blackened teeth, sharpened to a fine point like animals which were bared in a menacing snarl. Through their noses they wore two large feathers and their bodies were painted in various hues of scarlet and black paint, with particular attention paid to their faces.

Their hair was plastered down to their scalps with what seemed like orange mud from the forest floor itself. Jabuti craned his neck to look at the three white men who stood grinning lasciviously, with the sole exception of Alonso. As Jabuti looked at them he saw a tall man enter the crowd dressed in a spectacular head-dress and a robe, elaborately adorned with colourful feathers. Jabuti followed the man with his eyes as he walked into the parting crowd and up to a large, bubbling earthenware pot with angry flames licking its blackened sides. Suddenly he started to gyrate animatedly around the steaming cauldron as the crowd reached a higher pitch of excitement. Reaching into a large leather pouch he wore around his waist he threw various objects and powders into the boiling water. All the while he screeched and wailed in tongues that set Jabuti's nerves on edge as he watched the bizarre spectacle play out in front of his eyes.

Unconcerned for the pain it must have caused, the man thrust his hand into the water in one swift moment and the crowd hushed in an instant. As he withdrew his hand from the scalding waters the crowd let out a blood curdling cry, for in his grip he held the macabre spectacle of a man's severed head! His features were fixed in a permanent look of terror as he was released from his final indignity. Turning to face Jabuti, the man laughed maniacally, holding the deformed and grotesque object in front of him as Jabuti fainted from the intensity of the awful sight.

He awoke in a stinking damp hut with his head pounding and his racing heart reminded him of the terrible situation he was in. He tried to stand but his movements were restricted by ropes which bound his hands and ankles. His mouth felt stale and parched with the gag still in place and he found it an effort to breathe through his nose. Feeling trapped and scared in the darkness he fought against his bonds and thrashed around on the bare earth. Unable to hold his emotions in any longer he started to cry in desperation and he found his breathing becoming more and more difficult as his nose became blocked.

It can't end like this, will I never see my friends and my beloved Maru again? he thought. With those terrifying thoughts racing around his mind he heard hesitant footfalls coming from outside of the hut. Instinctively he shuffled into the corner of the hut and squeezed himself against the putrid smelling wall, hoping that the darkness might offer him some salvation. He saw a figure of a man enter with a lighted torch and Jabuti knew with finality that they had come for him and his pathetic attempt to remain hidden was for nothing. Jabuti looked on in alarm as he saw the man approach with a knife in his hand and he fought desperately against his bonds. As the figure got closer Jabuti realised that it was the fat white man he had met in the forest. Unnervingly he had a smile on his face as he crept closer and closer to Jabuti.

'No frighten, Jabuti, me friend,' he said with a flattened palm held against his chest as he untied Jabuti's gag. 'I come to free.'

'You are the one who spoke to me,' Jabuti said, recognising his voice in an instant.

Alonso nodded as he continued with his task.

'Why are you helping me?' Jabuti whispered.

'I no come your land for kill,' he said. 'I come as man of God, but…' he trailed off with sadness in his eyes.

'You are a man of God?' Jabuti asked with excitement in his eyes.

'I was,' he replied. 'No time talk, you leave now. They drunk asleep, you must go.'

'Will they not kill you?'

'Aah!' he said smiling, managing to find humour in the tense situation. 'They no like eat white men,' he said, patting his rotund midriff.

'Will you be in trouble for this?' Jabuti asked, raising his unshackled wrists.

'Jabuti, I fine. No worry me, go,' he said. It brought tears to Jabuti's eyes to see such compassion amongst all the evil things he had just witnessed as he looked at his smiling face.

Jabuti stood up to leave and looked to Alonso who just said softly, 'Go.'

Without looking back Jabuti fled, with the sound of his beating chest reverberating in his ears. He imagined at any moment to have his headlong flight arrested by spears and arrows flying around him in all directions. After a few minutes he managed to afford himself a little smile of relief as he rounded a corner only to find himself being knocked bodily onto the ground and heavily winded.

'Jabuti?!' came an astonished yet familiar voice.

Jabuti was unable to speak but smiled with relief as he saw Wanadi's surprised face looming down upon him. Wanadi pulled him up easily and into a fierce bear hug which did little to aid his breathing. He looked over Wanadi's shoulder to see Mapi approaching out of the shadows with a huge grin on his face.

'I'm so pleased to see you Jabuti.'

'Quick we have to run,' Jabuti managed to say, slowly getting his breath back.

'What is it?' Wanadi asked.

'Cannibals!'

'What?!' Mapi screamed.

'Shh!' Wanadi hissed.

'But…' Mapi said, rooted to the ground.

'But what Mapi? Get moving or else we're all dead,' Wanadi said, looking fiercely into his friend's shocked eyes. To his credit Mapi took only seconds to compose himself, immediately feeling ashamed of himself for endangering his friends.

'I'm sorry.'

No more time was wasted as they hastened their retreat. They had only been running for a few minutes when to their dread they heard shouts and wails coming from the distance.

'Run like you've never run before,' Wanadi shouted as they frantically picked up their pace. They ran through tangled undergrowth, past spiky thorns, never feeling the cuts and grazes inflicted upon them, such was the adrenaline they felt at being hunted down like wild animals. To their horror they found the voices suddenly getting closer and closer, just as their energy was beginning to wane.

'Listen, do you recognise that noise?' Mapi said as they came to a stop.

'Yes, cannibals,' Wanadi answered without a hint of sarcasm in his voice.

'No, over there,' Mapi protested, pointing to the sound.

'It's the river,' Jabuti exclaimed.

'Quick then, what are we waiting for? Let's make for it instead of waiting here to die,' Mapi said.

Despite the peril they faced, Jabuti and Wanadi still found the time to share a wry grin. They almost fell through the last remaining patch of forest and were met with the awe inspiring sight of the river in full flood. Their earlier optimism was replaced with a feeling of dismay as they considered their choices; death by drowning or being butchered by a bloodthirsty, baying mob.

CHAPTER ELEVEN

'What do we do Wanadi…Jabuti?' Mapi asked, looking upon the raging waters in front of them.

'Well, we either stand and fight,' Jabuti shouted above the roar of the river, 'or we take our chances in there.'

At that point a volley of arrows whistled past them, accompanied by the wild screams of their pursuers, who as yet were still hidden by the dense foliage.

'Come on there's no time to think about it,' Wanadi said.

Clambering over large rocks which lay between them and possible salvation, their progress was impaired by slippery algae which clung to its surface, ignorant of their need for haste. Finally they made it with precious little time to spare, for as they turned to take a look behind them they saw that the warriors were standing still and taking aim with their arrows. Jabuti spotted the two white men standing with a look of rage and fury upon their faces as Alonso looked on with a hapless expression. He had enough time to see the glint of the weapon that Diego held out in front of him, immediately seeing flames spill forth from its snout, accompanied by an enormous cracking sound seconds later.

'Jump!' Wanadi said as they reached the riverbank.

Just as they were making to jump into the frothing water they heard Mapi yelp out in pain, moments before they were swallowed up by the raging torrent. Upon resurfacing they were immediately swept away with such speed that within seconds the figures on the riverbank were just small dots on the horizon. Incredibly they remained together on the surface of the water but soon found themselves being thrashed around without mercy.

'Mapi?' Jabuti managed to shout above the noise as he saw his friend struggling.

'I think I've been hit,' he said through gritted teeth.

The two friends swam the short distance towards Mapi, linking arms together as they reached his side.

'Are you in pain Mapi?' Wanadi shouted, with a look of concern on his face.

'No I'll be fine, I just feel a bit weak that's all.'

'Well done my friend, just hang in there.'

Mapi managed a wan smile as he grimaced in pain.

'We need to make it to the water's edge, or else we'll never make it out of here,' Jabuti said. 'Can you make it Mapi? It's going to take all of our strength to fight the current.'

'I won't let you down.'

With that they swam as fast as their tired limbs could take them to the riverbank. No matter how hard they tried they just seemed to be treading water as they saw the vegetation fly by. But finally with a concerted effort they sensed that they were making headway, edging closer and closer, until they became distracted by a different kind of sound coming from the distance.

'What's that noise?' Mapi asked, looking around nervously.

With his words they turned to look downriver and they saw what looked to them like steam rising up in the distance. It took them a moment for the full impact of what they were seeing to hit them.

'Rapids!' Wanadi shouted.

Their progress towards the riverbank was halted as they felt themselves being pulled away from its safety and back into the swollen river. Seeing their lifeline receding before their eyes, they faced the terrifying prospect of being swept towards the rapids.

'I'm scared,' Mapi shouted out, barely making himself heard above the thunderous noise. 'What do we do Jabuti?'

'Just keep hanging onto each other and try to stay on top of the water.'

Just at that moment they were violently pulled from each other's grip by the force of the current. Jabuti thrashed about in the foaming river trying to look for his friends and turned to see a towering wall of water which pulled him towards it with such speed that he only had time to think about his own safety. Nearing the monstrous wave and fearing a lonely and uncomfortable demise, Wanadi and Mapi suddenly hove into view again and Jabuti immediately felt happy at seeing them, but also selfish to think that he would not die alone. He saw the terror in their faces as they were drawn inexorably towards it, but also when their eyes met there was a look of resignation on their faces.

How had it come to this, to have come so far and to be so cruelly robbed Jabuti thought? Before he knew it though he was sucked underneath the water with such violence that he had not had enough time to take a full breath. Being dragged further and further down into the inky blackness he started to panic. With the full weight of the water bearing down upon his chest he held what little precious air he had left in his lungs. Inexplicably though he found himself smiling as he felt a sense of calm wash over him. Before too long he felt himself blacking out, with images of Maru and a lifetime of friendship with his friends flashing through his mind.

Resigned to his fate he was suddenly and violently thrown out of the water with such force that when he landed the breath was knocked out of him. Determined not to be dragged down again he fought with all his remaining strength to stay on top of the water. His persistence paid off as the force of the rapids lessened and he floated gently away into calmer waters. To his relief he saw Wanadi and Mapi floating nearby looking exhausted. With what energy they had left they managed to swim to the safety of the riverbank, which they had fought for so valiantly, only moments earlier. Reaching the shallows they hauled their bedraggled bodies through the cloying, stinking mud and lay panting.

Jabuti immediately crawled over to Mapi to find he had passed out. He noticed a bloody angry hole which scored the upper part of his right thigh and through to the other side as thick blood oozed out.

'Wanadi, come here, help. We have to stop this bleeding,' he said, and they dragged him from the riverbank into the relative dryness of the forest.

'What could have caused it?' Wanadi asked, staring at the gaping hole.

'I don't know, but I heard a sound coming from that weapon that Diego was pointing at us,' Jabuti replied.

'Quick, press here,' Jabuti said as Wanadi bent down and pressed his hands around the wound to stem the blood loss.

'That's good Wanadi, I have to hunt for tools so that we can make a fire to close Mapi's injury.'

He searched for two bits of dry wood which was no easy task in the dampness of the rainforest, so that he could generate heat to make a fire. He gathered the implements as quick as he could and ran back to where Wanadi was still kneeling with his hands around Mapi's thigh.

'How is he doing?' Jabuti asked.

'He's lost a lot of blood but he's hanging in there.'

Kneeling down, Jabuti began turning the wood he had gathered in the palms of his hands into the other part until his hands began to ache and blister. Eventually faint wisps of smoke arose from the base and he carefully placed small bits of dry grass onto it, blowing gently into it. Spontaneously the little mound of dry grass burst into flames and he looked up at Wanadi, smiling with relief and satisfaction. Carefully he picked up the smouldering pile and transferred it into a larger mound of dry twigs, and before too long they had a raging fire going.

Jabuti then looked for a large pebble from the riverbank which they would have to heat in order to cauterise Mapi's wound. As it heated on the roaring fire he knelt by Mapi's head, gently squeezing water onto his forehead from water soaked moss. They both sat caring for their friend until the time came for Wanadi to carry the hot pebble over and place it on Mapi's wound. He gingerly carried it with a large forked stick which began to burn with the intense heat, knowing that even in his unconscious state Mapi would still feel the excruciating pain.

Jabuti's nostrils were immediately assaulted by a pungent smell of burning flesh as he looked down at his friend who squirmed with the pain. As Wanadi finished his task Jabuti went in search of the embauba tree whose large leaves held antiseptic properties. He felt selfish walking away, glad to be away from the awful smell and the guilt of seeing his friend suffer so much.

Knowing that he would find one growing by the river he identified it by the large cylindrical fruit which hung heavily laden with soft sweet flesh from its branches. Grabbing several of its large leaves he hurried quickly to Mapi's side, whereupon he wrapped them tightly around his wound so that they could do their job effectively. When all was done, Jabuti and Wanadi sat down, feeling stunned by the events of the last day.

'We're lucky to be alive,' Jabuti said after a period of silence.

'What happened back there?' Wanadi asked.

Jabuti took a deep breath and related all of the terrible events to Wanadi as he looked on in shock and amazement.

'I can't believe I was so stupid as to lead us into such danger,' Jabuti berated himself. 'Maybe it would be better for all of us if we returned home,' he said, poking a stick angrily into the fire.

'Stop that talk right now, we haven't come this far and been through all that we have experienced to just give up and walk back home with our tails between our legs,' Wanadi said. 'I couldn't live with myself if I let you return home with your dreams unfulfilled. I have been lucky enough to have two parents who have loved and cared for me all my life, I can't even begin to imagine your loss and how that might have affected you. No Jabuti, you have a dream and a yearning which must be fulfilled and I won't allow you to lose heart. When Mapi is well enough we will continue on our journey by your side, looking out for each other as we have always done.'

Jabuti sat staring into the glowing embers of the fire afterwards, feeling stunned at Wanadi's touching and heart-felt sentiments.

They awoke in the morning to the groans of Mapi who was beginning to stir.

'Mapi, can you hear me?' Jabuti asked.

'Where are we?' he replied as his eyelids fluttered weakly.

'We're downriver, about a day's walk from where we escaped.'

'So we're safe then?'

'Yes Mapi, we're safe.'

With a smile on his face he drifted off again into a deep sleep and Jabuti's mind turned to thoughts of food. Wanadi offered to look for some fish whilst Jabuti remained by Mapi's side. With the fire roaring and with Mapi sleeping soundly, Wanadi soon returned with two large gutted fish. Jabuti placed them on the fire and they sat back listening to its flesh sizzle and took in the pleasant aroma.

'I want them to pay for what they did to us,' Wanadi said, out of the blue, making Jabuti jump.

'Wanadi, don't say that.'

'Why not, are you frightened?' he mocked.

'Yes, of course I am, I'm not ashamed to say. How can we go up against a band of bloodthirsty cannibals?'

'I'm not talking about them, I would be frightened of that as well. I'm talking about just the white men.'

'But we are not killers Wanadi, what would that make us if we sought revenge?' he asked. 'Don't forget that the only reason I'm alive is thanks to the fat one, Alonso.'

'I don't want to kill them Jabuti, you should know me better than that,' he said. 'I just want to make them pay somehow for what they did. Alonso will be safe, you owe your life to him. They will be back in the forest again I'm sure, looking for some more fools like us to make an offering to that tribe.'

'I don't know Wanadi…' Jabuti paused, 'Alonso did say though that he had been a man of God, maybe he could tell us something useful.'

'Well we know where their village is now and if we travel at night we'll have more cover. Then we wait a safe distance for the white men to show themselves and follow them when they leave,' Wanadi said with confidence.

'I've already risked your lives by bringing you along on my selfish quest.'

'You didn't bring us along. We offered, remember?'

'You know I can't argue when you're like this Wanadi. Let's wait and see what Mapi says when he's well enough.'

'I agree with Wanadi,' Mapi said.

'Mapi, how long have you been awake?' Jabuti asked.

'Long enough to know that Wanadi talks sense. I know you feel guilty about leading us into danger, but I've never felt so alive in my whole life; despite the danger.'

'That's settled then,' Wanadi said, giving Mapi a wink.

'By the way what exactly did happen to you?' Mapi asked, and Jabuti had to relive the whole terrible saga once more.

They stayed put for several more days, resting and creating more weapons, including bows and arrows which they daubed with the powerful curare poison. They constructed hammocks for each of them from vines and straw matting which were folded neatly and carried on their backs. With their tasks completed and with Mapi almost back to full strength they felt satisfied with their endeavours. Food was prepared for their journey to avoid lighting fires for fear of being spotted. They sat down afterwards in the early evening for a full meal of roasted fish, monkey, fresh yams and mango.

'Are we sure about this?' Jabuti asked one final time.

'Stop worrying about us Jabuti,' Wanadi replied.

'Stop talking ladies, let's go!' Mapi said, standing up on his fast healing leg.

CHAPTER TWELVE

They decided to keep to the side of the river to avoid any more nasty surprises in the deep forest, but that meant that they had to negotiate their way carefully around rocks and large boulders, thick with algae and moss. It actually took two days of hard endeavour on all their parts as for several hours they were forced to move on their hands and knees numerous times around the boulder-strewn terrain. It was particularly hard for Mapi who found the going hard, due to his injured leg.

Several times he slipped, landing hard upon his injury but with fortitude he continued, his features contorted in pain. With nerves on edge they crept closer and closer towards the spot where they were forced to jump into the river. With every strange noise and movement Jabuti felt his heart leap into his mouth, fearing that they would encounter the cannibals again. They arrived at their destination just as dawn was breaking, relieved to have survived that far unscathed. They chose a spot with the defence of a barrier of rocks behind them and Jabuti took the time to refresh himself in the river with his friends. Feeling invigorated they sat in the warmth of the sun's rays drying off and followed it by a quick breakfast. Knowing that they would need their strength and alertness for later they took turns in sleeping, with Jabuti taking the first watch.

He sat thinking how much they had been through already and of the dangers they had faced. With no one to talk to his mind began to wander to thoughts of Maru again and of how much he missed her. Throwing pebbles into the water he watched them skim the surface and wondered if she was sitting by the river thinking about him also. Suddenly he heard voices coming from nearby making him realise how much he had been distracted by his thoughts. Climbing to the top of the boulder he spotted the three white men walking to the edge of the river to fill up their water containers and they knelt to splash water on their faces. He scanned the edge of the forest keenly for signs of the warriors and for a second he felt nervous that they were just trying to lure them out of their hiding spot.

Watching them as they knelt by the river chatting, he realised that he had been worrying unnecessarily for they seemed to be acting normally. Sliding over to his sleeping partners he gently woke them up, motioning for them to be quiet with a finger to his pursed lips. They followed him to the vantage point with their eyes widening when they saw what Jabuti pointed out to them.

'So what do we do now?' Mapi whispered.

'We give them time to enter the forest, then we follow.'

'How do we know what they are doing, they might just return back to the camp,' Mapi said.

'No, I think they're setting off for the day because I saw them filling up their water bottles. And they have full back packs,' Jabuti answered.

Jabuti sat motionless with his friends and continued to watch the white men until they finally arose from the riverbank and set off into the forest in a different direction to which they had arrived. Waiting several moments longer the three friends gathered up their belongings and tentatively followed them. They found their messy trail which led them deep into the forest on a determined course, to a place known only to the white men. They stopped some time later at a small clearing and the friends crept up and watched them, hidden by the undergrowth.

'What do you think they're doing?' Mapi asked in a whisper.

'I'm not sure,' Wanadi replied, 'but I say we ambush them here.'

'And then what Wanadi?' Jabuti asked. 'I want to see where they're going and what they're up to.'

It seemed like they had stopped for the benefit of Alonso who sat with his head between his knees, visibly wheezing and sweating. During that time the man called Diego stood with his hands on his hips looking impatient as he scanned the forest with his keen eyes. Jabuti's heart stopped and he held his breath, feeling sure that Diego's eyes had locked onto his as he stood peering into the gloom. Although Jabuti felt confident that there was no way he could be seen he still felt a shiver run down his spine as he looked into the man's confident gaze. Eventually Diego looked away and barked something at Alonso and Jabuti let out his breath. Alonso eventually got to his feet when Diego roughly pushed him in the small of his back and he turned to look at him with a look of menace that Jabuti hadn't noticed in him before. The two disparate groups continued on their trek for the best part of the morning until the white men began to slow their pace and Jabuti and his friends took shelter in a good vantage point. Jabuti's gaze followed them as they walked into a clearing and he gasped audibly as his eyes rested upon a sight he had never encountered before in his life.

The friends looked on in amazement at a colossal structure which seemed to grow from the forest floor itself. Their eyes rested upon an immense, ancient temple which rose high above them and up into the forest canopy itself. Symmetrical on each of its three sides it had large steps around the sides of the structure and smaller steps rising up through the middle. Perched high upon the object was a flat-roofed structure with open windows and a doorway. Jabuti gazed on in horror and astonishment at grotesque carvings of men's faces in various states of terror and intense pain. The haunting figures were balanced though by beautiful swirls and intricate markings etched into the stone. The forest seemed to resent the building's intrusion into its world as it slowly reclaimed its territory, with vines and creepers exploring every nook and crevice.

'What is that?' Mapi asked.

'I don't know, but I don't like the look of it,' Wanadi replied.

'Let's just watch them and see what they do next,' Jabuti said.

Jabuti and his friends took the chance to have some water and food whilst they sat on their vigil. After some time Diego stood up and roughly pushed the other two off their platform and barked at them. They stood up reluctantly and began walking around the clearing searching in the undergrowth on their hands and knees. Meanwhile Diego stood with both hands on his hips and a look of annoyance on his face as they rifled through the forest litter.

'What are they doing?' Mapi asked.

'Don't ask such stupid questions Mapi, how should we know?' Wanadi snapped back.

'Hey tha—' Mapi protested.

'Be quiet both of you,' interrupted Jabuti.

Jabuti sat in silence with his companions, feeling tense with the stress of the situation, wondering what their next move would be. Just at that moment Miguel leapt up from the forest floor, shouting as he held an object aloft in his hands. Diego put down his weapon and immediately rushed over to his side and grabbed it off him, furiously brushing off the dirt and grime which stubbornly clung to its surface. As the object was cleaned Diego's eyes grew wider and wider as he turned the object over and over in his hands. To Jabuti the yellowish looking object seemed to glint in the occasional shafts of sunlight which pierced the forest canopy. It held the form of an animal not dissimilar to the wood carvings that Jabuti made himself. Looking at it he became awestruck at the skill it must have taken to create an object so beautiful.

The three friends looked at each other in confusion as Diego and Miguel danced around, laughing and clapping each other on the shoulders, but Alonso stood looking on at the impromptu celebration with a dejected look.

'I don't want to ask a stupid question again,' Mapi said cautiously, unsure of his friends' response, 'But what's going on?'

Despite the tenseness of the situation both Jabuti and Wanadi couldn't help but laugh at Mapi's question.

'I don't know Mapi,' Wanadi said, smiling as he ruffled his hair. 'But whatever it is, it holds great importance for them.'

'So what do we do, just sit here and watch them all day?' Mapi asked.

'Well I don't know what we should do, maybe it was a mistake to follow them here,' Jabuti replied.

'Remember what they tried to do to us?' Wanadi countered.

'Yes I know Wanadi, but is revenge really the right thing to seek?'

'We've talked about it before Jabuti, if we don't scare them off in some way how do we know we won't meet them on our way back home?'

'What do you plan to do then?'

'Well first of all we need to get our hands on that weapon that Diego holds by his side all of the time. He's not holding it now, maybe this is our only chance.'

'One of us needs to get it then,' Mapi said.

'Do you want to do it?' Wanadi asked of him.

'Yes, I want to do my part for what they did to me,' Mapi said with steely determination.

'Don't you think that was hasty?' Jabuti asked as Mapi crept away.

'I think we can trust him by now Jabuti. And if we don't get hold off that weapon right now we might miss our chance,' Wanadi replied.

With Mapi gone the two of them sat looking out at the clearing where the white men were still on their hands and knees, searching through the leaves and detritus.

Several agonising moments later Jabuti's attention was drawn to the edge of the clearing to where Mapi had emerged from the cover of the forest, creeping to where the weapon lay. Mapi reached out for the weapon and kept one eye on the white men as he did so. So concerned was he in looking at them that he misjudged his reach and the weapon clattered onto the stone structure, making a noise so loud it made Jabuti jump.

Jabuti looked over to where the three white men were standing and he saw the look of shock in their eyes. Mapi remained frozen to the spot as he watched Miguel suddenly start running towards him. Still holding the weapon Mapi raised it in a defensive gesture and the forest erupted in an explosion so loud it made his ears ring.

Jabuti and Wanadi stared in disbelief as they saw Miguel tumble to the ground with his arms and legs flailing. Looking equally surprised was Miguel, as he stared down at his stomach to see a ragged, gaping hole with blood and guts spewing out from within.

Clutching his abdomen in a vain attempt to push his innards back in he sank to his knees, looking towards Mapi with a look of astonishment in his eyes and uttered two final words; *'Dios myo!'*

CHAPTER THIRTEEN

Alonso stood holding a smoking weapon as Diego looked at him with surprise at the speed with which he had grabbed one of his two remaining weapons. Snapping out of his shock he raised his remaining weapon to fire at Alonso just as Wanadi threw his spear and sent it flying towards him. Diego felt the rush of wind rush past his face as it narrowly missed his head. He turned rapidly to see Jabuti and Wanadi running towards him with their bows drawn, aimed squarely at his chest. He stood for a moment confused and unsure of what to do, but he quickly turned on his heels and fled into the cover of the forest.

'Alonso,' Jabuti said as he approached him, warily.

'Jabuti,' he replied, hand outstretched in greeting.

Jabuti took it and held him by the forearm in a firm grip, 'Thank you,' was all Jabuti said, looking solemnly into his eyes.

'He evil man, I no like,' he said, looking at Miguel's bloodied corpse. 'I no think I see you again Jabuti.'

Jabuti smiled warmly and introduced Wanadi and Mapi to him as they joined them and they thanked

Alonso for his bravery in setting their friend free. He said that Diego wasn't happy as they had made trouble for him with the tribe. Diego told the tribe that he would set off into the forest to look for another sacrifice to make amends.

'What is this place?' Wanadi asked.

'It place of God for tribes, old, very old.'

'And that?' Wanadi asked, indicating the object which lay by the side of Miguel's prostrate form.

'It called *oro* in my language, make men powerful.'

'How so?' Mapi asked.

'*Oh madre mia,*' he replied. 'How I say?' He then began to show with sign language and a smattering of words how jewellery and fine ornaments were made from it.

'So you come to our land for this *oro*?' Jabuti asked, repeating the strange sounding word.

'No, no I come for God but I…' he paused, 'I meet Diego and Miguel, they tell of *oro*, I stupid…' His words trailed off with a faraway look in his eyes.

'And what about that tribe?' Wanadi asked.

'Diego bring sacrifice, they show here, we take *oro*. I sorry…' he said with tears in his eyes.

Even though he had helped save his life Jabuti couldn't help but feel angry that he had been part of their evil plan. However Alonso had also turned his back on his wicked friends and as such he could be forgiven, Jabuti thought.

'You know Jabuti's father Pedro, he was a man of God?' Mapi asked, breaking the silence.

'Pedro,' he mused. 'Your father?!'

'Yes,' Jabuti replied.

At his reply Alonso stepped forward and hugged Jabuti, 'This what God want for me, to help you,' he said, his face transforming as it lit up with a warm smile.

'So you knew my father?' Jabuti asked with hope in his eyes.

'Yes Jabuti, your father was a goo—' his words ended abruptly in a deafening boom. He lurched forward violently with the force of the explosion, clutching his chest as blood seeped through his fingers.

Amongst the shock and sudden brutality of the situation Jabuti briefly glimpsed Diego's evil face grinning at him from within the folds of the forest's greenery as he slinked away; leaving behind a scene of utter devastation.

'Alonso!' Jabuti screamed, cradling his head in his hands as he lay dying.

'Jabuti, I happy,' he managed to say through the pain. 'I bad man but God smile me, I see him now,' he said, gazing serenely at the forest canopy at some unseen deity. 'He calls me,' he gasped, raising his arm weakly as if reaching out to the sky itself.

'Oh Alonso…' Jabuti said, looking tenderly into his eyes, touched by the tenderness of a man he hardly knew.

'No cry Jabuti,' he whispered, raising his hand to touch Jabuti's face.

Jabuti took Alonso's hand and kissed it, watching him as he passed peacefully away into the arms of a God he had so deeply yearned for. Touched by the tragic, yet touching scene, Wanadi and Mapi stood with tears in their eyes.

'He's gone Jabuti,' Wanadi said to him as he sat cradling Alonso's lifeless body.

'I know,' he looked up with sad eyes. 'I didn't know him but I feel moved by what he did for us.'

'He was a brave warrior Jabuti, he died a good death.'

'What shall we do with him Jabuti?' Mapi asked.

'He was looking towards the trees as he died, it's like he thought his God lived up there. I think we should help him on his journey and lay him to rest there,' Jabuti said, pointing to the top of the temple.

Without further discussion they gently carried Alonso's body to the top of the temple and placed him on a flat slab of stone inside the open doorway. Once completed, they stood around awkwardly, not sure of what to do next.

'Should we say something Jabuti?' Mapi asked.

'Yes Mapi I think we should,' Jabuti replied, smiling warmly at his friend. He took a moment to compose himself, and began, 'I call to the white men's God to take the body of Alonso. He was a brave and kind man who died helping us, we will always think of you Alonso, we will never forget what you did for us.' They held hands and looked down at Alonso who rested with a peaceful look upon his face.

They slowly climbed down the stone steps and came to rest on the bottom tier, and tried to make sense of everything that had just happened. Feeling uncomfortable with the bloody sight of Miguel's body they dragged his body further into the forest, out of sight.

'Alonso was beginning to tell you about your father Jabuti,' Mapi said after they had returned from their grisly chore.

'I know,' Jabuti replied, looking dejected.

'Until that evil man Diego took his life,' Wanadi said with anger in his eyes. 'I say we go after him.'

'No Wanadi.'

'But w—'

'No,' Jabuti interrupted. 'No, just leave him Wanadi. We don't need to worry about him any more.'

Wanadi opened his mouth to protest but he soon realised the futility of it.

Eventually they succumbed to sleep, exhausted by the day's events and Jabuti felt glad to be leaving in the morning from a place which he felt was cursed. He drifted off into a deep sleep, glad to feel its warm embrace soothe his troubled mind. However he was wrenched abruptly from his slumbers by a low, growling sound coming from deep within the forest which set his nerves on edge. He was about to awaken his companions but saw they were fully awake also.

'It's a jaguar Mapi,' Wanadi whispered, just as Mapi was opening his mouth to ask the question.

'What is it doing?' he asked.

'It's eating Miguel,' Wanadi said, straight-faced.

'What?!' he shouted much too loudly.

'Shh, Mapi,' Wanadi said. 'Do you want to be next?'

'Maybe we should leave now before it comes for us?'

'No Mapi,' Jabuti joined in. 'We're safe here by the fire, it won't come near us.'

That being said though Jabuti offered to keep the first watch and his friends tentatively returned to their slumbers. Jabuti sat with his senses on full alert, the sound of cracking bones and tearing flesh carrying through the still forest air. Eventually Wanadi came to his side, relieving him of his watch and between all three of them they managed to make it unscathed through to the morning; albeit bleary-eyed and with nerves on edge.

As they were packing up to leave, Wanadi looked towards the object which had caused so much suffering the day before.

'I know what you're thinking Wanadi, we should leave it,' Jabuti said. 'We have no need for it; it has spilt so much blood already.'

'I know but what if we can use it in some way. These white men have shown already how much it means to them, if we have no need for it then we just throw it back into the forest,' he said with his usual pragmatism.

Jabuti couldn't really argue with him as it made sense to him. If they could use it for whatever reason then it could make dealing with the white men a lot easier he thought.

'What shall we do with those?' Mapi asked, pointing to the two weapons which were left on the forest floor.

'I think we should take them,' Wanadi said.

'No Wanadi, have we not seen enough death already?' Jabuti said.

'But we could use them,' he protested.

'Jabuti makes sense Wanadi, we have no need of weapons like that.'

Despite himself Wanadi knew there was no point in arguing with his friends and he decided to respect their wishes. With a final look back at the place which would be forever etched into their memories they turned their backs and continued on their journey.

CHAPTER FOURTEEN

The atmosphere was sombre for the next week as they continued on their journey, with little being said between them. Jabuti thought it best to remain patient and hope that within time the atmosphere would lighten. The mood wasn't helped much either by the constant fear of running into the cannibals again. However, they lessened their chances of being spotted by travelling at night, and taking it in turns to keep a lookout during the daylight hours. Within time they had managed to put a safe distance between themselves and their terrible encounter. Feeling more relaxed the atmosphere changed imperceptibly at first with the conversation flowing more freely, until they were chatting amongst themselves as if nothing had happened.

Jabuti was more concerned about how the recent drama would affect Mapi, for he was the most sensitive of the three. But much to his surprise he was soon back to his normal self, bickering good naturedly with Wanadi. With another day coming to an end they set up camp as they had done countless times before and Wanadi offered to go fishing for supper. Whilst he was gone Jabuti and Mapi started making a fire, safe in the knowledge that they were far away from any danger, however they still remained alert. With

Jabuti's stomach beginning to rumble he wondered why it was taking so long for Wanadi to return. Just as he was thinking about going to look for him, Wanadi returned into the camp with a look of astonishment on his face.

'That must have been a big one that got away Wanadi,' he said, referring to his empty hands.

'I have just seen a vision of beauty,' he replied, out of breath.

'Ri-gh-t,' Jabuti said, sharing a quizzical look with Mapi. 'I'll go along with you, so exactly how big was this fish?'

'I haven't been fishing, I got to the river and just stood there transfixed by what I saw.'

'I think he's been on the Sar again,' Mapi quipped.

'Come on Wanadi sit down you're not making any sense,' Jabuti said, leading his friend by the elbow towards the fire. Wanadi sat down and looked properly at his friends for the first time since entering the camp.

'Sorry I know I'm acting strange it's just that when I got to the river I heard all this laughing and splashing, so I crouched down and made my way closer to where the commotion was coming from,' he said as they listened intently. 'Then I saw the most beautiful group of girls I have ever laid eyes upon, underneath a waterfall washing themselves. I tell you it was the most mesmerising thing I have ever seen.'

'Naked girls?' Mapi asked, wide-eyed.

'Yes Mapi, completely naked,' Wanadi replied with a boyish grin.

Coming from a conservative society where women quite freely walked around with bare breasts but always with lower garments to cover their modesty, they had limited knowledge as to what lay beneath.

'Did they see you?' Jabuti asked.

'No I just lay there looking,' Wanadi sniggered.

'Wanadi!' Jabuti said, laughing as well.

'What were they like?' Mapi asked.

'I can't really explain, you'll have to see them for yourself.'

'Can we go and have a look Jabuti?' Mapi asked, jumping up in eagerness.

'I don't know.'

'Come on Jabuti, they didn't look like cannibals to me.'

'Oh, alright but we need to be careful.'

Despite himself Jabuti experienced a sense of excitement, but also a little guilty for going to stare at some naked women whilst Maru waited patiently back home for him. They crept silently towards the edge of the small waterfall and carefully peered over. Like Wanadi they stared in wonder at the girls who were frolicking about in the water, unaware of their presence.

In Wanadi's eagerness to get a better look he crept closer to the side of the waterfall and inadvertently loosened a rock which was sent crashing down into the water below.

'Who's there?' they heard one of the girls immediately cry out.

'Shh!' the friends said to each other, crouching even lower.

'I said who's there?' she called out more firmly.

'Oh no, we're in trouble now,' Wanadi said as he stood up.

'No Wanadi!' they both called out to him.

Standing brazenly with hands on her hips, the one who spoke looked at Wanadi and turned to her three friends, 'Wow, what a fine specimen,' she said as her friends stood naked as the day they were born.

Wanadi remained standing and shifted nervously on his feet, not sure where to look.

'Are you alone stranger?'

'Erm... no,' he replied as Jabuti and Mapi got to their feet and waved at them sheepishly, feeling a bit ridiculous.

'So you've gone all shy now that we've found your hiding spot?' she teased as her friends fell about giggling. 'Come down then and introduce yourselves, don't worry we'll cover up to spare your blushes.'

Feeling embarrassed and guilty the three friends climbed gingerly down the side of the small waterfall, careful not to slip on the slimy algae. When they reached the bottom they turned to face the girls as they emerged from the river, showing long slender legs and lithe tight bodies. The confident one had startling green eyes the colour of the forest foliage itself, with full and pouting lips. The other two were equally beautiful with a grace and inner calm in the way they carried themselves.

Jabuti and his friends actually gasped at being confronted by such a sight of pure wonder. Wanadi for one was disappointed when they climbed into loin cloths, but he knew that conversation would have been virtually impossible if they hadn't.

'What are you doing here, I've never seen you before?' the one who did all the talking asked.

'We're here to l—' Wanadi began to say.

'To learn more about the forest and all the secrets it holds,' Jabuti said, interrupting him.

'I see, intrepid travellers eh? Well you must come to our village and rest, you must be tired from your travels.'

'Well I need to talk it over with my friends, we'll be missed by our village if we stay away too long,' Jabuti replied.

They walked a small distance away to confer.

'Why did you say that Jabuti, have you seen what they look like?' Wanadi said, craning to look over his shoulder.

'Yes come on Jabuti, what danger could they hold for us?' Mapi added.

'I'm not saying they're dangerous, but we need to be careful especially after what happened last time.'

'Well they look harmless to me and I can't see where they could hide any weapons,' Wanadi said, giggling and nudging Mapi.

'Hmm, alright but be careful that's all I say.'

'Great, come on,' Wanadi said.

They returned to the group of girls as introductions were made all round, finding out that the confident one was called Samampo.

'So what were you doing here?' Wanadi asked, making nervous conversation.

'We were washing ourselves, I thought that would have been obvious from your hiding spot' she replied, watching him with an amused grin on her face.

'Well I wasn't really watching you as such it's just that er, well I …'

'It's alright I'm just teasing you, we're not shy about showing our bodies. We come from a very giving and open society, as you'll find out,' she replied, laughing along with her friends.

'Are you coming with us then?' she asked.

Jabuti's friends looked towards him for confirmation and he just shrugged his shoulders and they grinned from ear to ear.

Upon entering the village Jabuti was immediately struck by the beauty and order of the place. Flowers abounded in various colours and different hues, and of varieties he had never seen before. The paths were formed in straight lines with wood shavings scattered along them, leading up to neatly arranged huts. To Jabuti the whole place looked clean with a fresh perfume emanating from all the flowers dotted around the compound. This is completely different to anything I've ever seen before he thought, as he looked towards his friends who were also staring around in wonderment. They were led through the village, being greeted warmly by a throng of women varying in ages from young girls to old women.

'What's wrong Mapi?' Jabuti asked as he saw him looking around with a furrowed brow.

'There aren't any men, it's just women and girls,' Mapi whispered.

'They must be out hunting,' Wanadi replied.

'But there aren't any old men or boys either, they wouldn't all be out hunting.'

'Well there must be some, maybe they have different customs to us. They could all be busy doing something together,' Jabuti said. 'Let's not abuse their hospitality by questioning them, look they're beginning to look at us,' he said as Samampo noticed them conferring in hushed tones.

'Is everything alright?' she asked with a smile.

'Oh, yes everything is fine. We were just saying how everything is so neat and ordered in your village,' Jabuti replied.

'Oh yes, well us women like it this way, so pretty don't you think?'

'Yes, very. I hope us men won't mess it up for you,' Jabuti said with an attempt at humour.

'Oh there's no chance of that,' she replied with a serious look.

'What did she mean by that?' Mapi whispered, moving closer to Jabuti and Wanadi.

'Nothing Mapi, I just think it's just her way,' Wanadi said.

'Let us offer you something to eat and drink, you must be tired after your travels. Kachiri, Tatuie look after them will you,' she said to her friends.

'Come Jabuti, I will walk with you,' she said, linking her arm with his and Jabuti felt instantly guilty, thinking of Maru.

They were led to a structure with open sides, thatch matting for a roof and a fire blazing away. Jabuti noticed freshly caught fish of a variety he had never noticed before and vegetables of a quality and size which made his mouth water. After weeks of trudging through the forest, living mostly off monkey meat and the occasional bit of fruit it looked like a veritable feast to Jabuti.

'I see you're hungry,' Samampo said, noticing the way in which he looked in wonder at the spread laid out before them. 'We women are very resourceful.'

'There she goes again,' Mapi muttered to Jabuti.

'Mapi, you have a question?' Samampo asked.

'Oh it's nothing,' Mapi muttered, feeling like he had been caught out. 'We seem to be the only men here.'

'Yes you do,' she said flatly.

Unsure as to whether she was joking or not the three friends just sat looking at her impassive features. Feeling uncomfortable with the silence Mapi started laughing with Jabuti and Wanadi soon joining in as the women sat with thin smiles. With night drawing in the conversation flowed more freely as the three friends sat down for dinner, being ably and courteously served by their hosts. Despite himself Jabuti tried not to stare at the women seated around him who tended to his every whim, as he had never before encountered such beautiful and sensuous women. Looking across to where Wanadi and Mapi were sitting he saw that they too were enraptured by the attention they were receiving. The evening became even more entrancing when several of the women stood up to dance around the fire, moving sensually to the clapping of hands.

After their recent troubles the evening was a welcome break. With their meal over and despite their glorious surroundings the friends found themselves yawning from all the hardships they had suffered. Samampo brought the evening to a close, offering them the opportunity to rest up for the night in one of their dwellings. Reluctant to sleep out in the open again for another night they gladly accepted her kind invitation.

'This is very generous of you,' Jabuti said as she led them to a hut which had been specially prepared for them, with candles burning from animal fat and flower petals floating in wooden pots. Upon entering Jabuti noticed how fresh it smelt compared to the hut he had to share with Wanadi and Mapi back home.

'Rest here,' she said, turning with a flourish and left a lingering smell of perfume.

The three of them just sat looking at each other at the unexpected turn of events in their day.

'Well I never imagined this when I awoke this morning,' Wanadi said.

'Me neither,' Mapi replied.

'I think it's strange that there are no men in the village,' Mapi repeated.

'We've discussed that already Mapi, they're out on a hunting party probably,' Wanadi replied, exasperated.

'What all of them?' he protested.

'Yes why not, they co—' Wanadi began.

'Look shut up will you both and go to sleep,' Jabuti said interrupting him, smiling and rolling his eyes at the same time.

'It's just strange that's all I'm saying,' muttered Mapi as Wanadi flicked him on the ear.

'Ow! Jabuti, do you see what he's doing to me?'

Jabuti groaned as he listened to his two friends bickering good naturedly between themselves.

CHAPTER FIFTEEN

After a night in which Jabuti slept more soundly than he could remember in recent times, he was awoken by Samampo, bearing a plate of freshly cut fruit.

'I hope you slept well?' she asked her guests, who were in various states of wakefulness.

'There was no need to go to the trouble of bringing us breakfast, we could have joined you,' Jabuti said.

'Breakfast!' she laughed. 'It is breakfast for you, the sun is already high up in the sky, we have begun to prepare lunch already.'

'I'm so sorry,' Jabuti said, embarrassed at having put their hosts out.

'There's no need to worry,' she replied sweetly. 'Take your time, you must be tired after your travels, join us when you're ready.' With that she left the three friends alone.

They quickly ate the fruit and went in search of Samampo. They found her cooking with others of the village and asked if they could be of any assistance.

'You can start by having a wash, you stink,' she said with the mischievous grin of hers that they had begun to notice all too well. For the first time since leaving their village Jabuti became aware of their appearance with their dirty faces, scratched arms and torsos from trekking through the forest. Normally they would bathe daily in the refreshing waters of the river but so consumed had they become by their goal that they had not bathed for a long time.

'Sorry,' Jabuti said, feeling a bit embarrassed.

'You are amongst friends Jabuti, there is no need to apologise. Here take some of this soap, go and have a good wash and when you return we'll have lunch prepared,' she said, offering them a wooden bowl containing a thick brownish liquid used for washing. The mixture was easily prepared by boiling the soap nuts from the sapindus tree which when cooled produced an effective cleanser that was used in a variety of purposes.

'Thank you,' Jabuti said, taking the bowl of soap and left with his friends towards the river.

'I didn't really want to mention it, but you do stink, Jabuti. I've been meaning to say something for days now,' Wanadi quipped.

'And you smell as fresh as an orchid,' Jabuti joked back.

They arrived at the river and walked into it with the water flowing refreshingly around their tired and aching limbs. They swam the short distance to the waterfall where they lathered their hair and bodies and stood underneath it, feeling invigorated with its strength as it crashed all around them. When they had finished they lay on a comforting bed of lush, green grass by the riverbank, letting themselves dry from the warming sun's rays. Reluctantly they prised their aching bodies from their comfortable spot and returned to the village.

'Well look at you three, you look like different men,' Samampo said with a pleased expression upon her face. 'Sit, have some lunch.'

'I feel a bit guilty,' Jabuti said. 'You have gone to all of this trouble for us and we have nothing to offer in return.'

'Oh you will,' she said, regarding him with an amused expression.

Mapi nudged Jabuti at her comment but he studiously ignored him, not wanting to look his way.

'So where is the rest of your tribe?' Mapi asked. 'The village seems a bit empty.'

'They're on a hunting trip, they should be back any time soon,' Samampo replied.

'Oh I see, that explains it,' Mapi said.

'Explains what?' she asked, her curiosity piqued.

'Oh nothing,' Jabuti interjected.' We were just wondering, that's all.'

With their lunch finished the conversation turned to their reason for being so far from home. Feeling comfortable enough in their presence Jabuti began to tell them his story. Their hosts sat there open mouthed at his tale, especially when he came to the part where they fought raging rapids to escape the cannibals. Jabuti left out the part as to what happened to the three white men though.

'Jabuti, you have suffered so much in your life,' Samampo said.

'Well, you get used to it and learn to live with it.' He replied with an attempt at a smile.

'Well it will be our pleasure to look after you for as long as you wish to stay here,' she said.

Jabuti and his friends offered to help them clear up but they were told to just sit and relax. With nothing else to do they retired to their hut where they sat chatting until dusk began to descend. After a while they became aware of animated chatter coming from outside so they peeked out to see what the commotion was all about. Stepping outside they saw a group of women emerging from the forest with monkeys strung over their shoulders and a huge pig slung underneath two poles.

As the new arrivals were being fussed over Jabuti saw them look their way with an initial look of concern, but to his relief he saw it change to one of warmth as they smiled at Jabuti and his friends.

'I told you there were no men,' said Mapi in hushed tones. 'What kind of society has women who go out hunting?'

'Shh! Mapi,' Jabuti said. 'It is a bit strange I must admit, but let's not offend them. Give them time to settle in then maybe all will be explained later.'

'Yes Mapi, don't spoil it for me with Kachiri,' Wanadi said. 'I think she likes me,' he said with a wink.

They stood as the hunting party approached them and Jabuti felt uncomfortable when he found himself being scrutinised by one of the older women as she neared him. He tried not to return her penetrating stare but he felt himself being inexplicably drawn back to her inquisitive eyes.

Even at a distance he saw that her eyes held a sense of calm with lines etched around them, suggesting a sense of wisdom and a life lived to the full. She held herself proudly as she walked, with the accompanying group following her wake as in deference to her. She had a thick mane of long, silvery-grey hair which was pulled back from her face and held at the nape of her neck by a leather band, allowing it to fall and swing gracefully down her back. She had a wry smile on her face not dissimilar to the one that Samampo always seemed to have.

'This is my mother, Nakwatcha,' Samampo said.

'Mother this is Jabuti, Wanadi and Mapi. They have come to stay with us for a while.'

'Jabuti, Jabuti,' she mumbled to herself, her eyes staring off into the distance as if lost in a dream. 'It can't be!' she said, suddenly brought back into the present.

'Mother, what is it?'

'Jabuti, I can't believe I have met you after all this time.'

'I don't understand,' Jabuti replied, feeling uncertain as to what was happening.

'I knew it from the moment I saw you from the forest, I just had to look into your eyes to be sure.'

Wanadi and Mapi exchanged puzzled looks, glancing towards Jabuti who was visibly sweating and nervous in her presence.

'You have your mother's eyes!

'My mother's eyes?!' Jabuti exclaimed. 'How do you know about my mother? She died giving birth to me.'

'No Jabuti, I have met your mother. She is very much alive, or she was the last time I saw her.'

'What kind of cruel joke is this, how could you know her? We have travelled for many moons to reach your lands; it is impossible.'

'Yes, what is going on?' Wanadi asked, leaping to Jabuti's defence.

'Jabuti, be calm I wish you no harm. What I say is true, please believe me.'

'Jabuti, I have never known my mother to lie,' Samampo said. 'She is our leader and has our best interests at heart, please listen to her.'

Dumbstruck, Jabuti sat down with his friends, listening with a sceptical mind to what she had to say.

'Jabuti, I am the leader of this village and my people's wellbeing is my utmost concern and that of our guests too,' she began in earnest. 'I know it will come as a shock to you, but believe me when I tell you, I have met your mother.' Jabuti looked over at his friends with raised eyebrows as she began her tale.

'One day whilst out foraging for wood, we came across a bedraggled form lying on the forest floor, half-starved and close to death. We picked up this poor creature and carried her back to our village where we tenderly cared for her and brought her gently back to life.

'Slowly she regained her strength, but she steadfastly refused to speak to us. She used to sit sat staring continuously into the forest, as if searching for something or someone to emerge from its shadows.

Eventually she began to contribute to village life and started helping out with chores. We all got used to this silent but graceful creature being in our midst and her refusal to speak became less of an issue and we decided to let it be.'

'But how do you know it was my mother?' Jabuti said to her, feeling a growing sense of irritation and suspicion.

'Patience Jabuti, all will be explained,' she replied.

'I've been patient all of my life!' Jabuti exploded. 'I'm not going to sit here listening to this nonsense, my mother is dead. Why would you lie to me?' he said, springing to his feet in frustration and anger.

'Jabuti, calm down,' Wanadi said as he put a comforting arm around his friend. 'Let's listen to what Nakwatcha has to say, we have come so far not to listen.'

'Jabuti I know it is painful for you but you have to trust me.'

Seeing that Jabuti had begun to calm down she continued with her tale, 'One day whilst working in the garden with your mother she turned to me and told me that she once had a child. I was shocked to hear her speak after so long and once she started the words just came pouring out. We just sat there and I listened to her talk and talk as the tears streamed down her face.

The tale she began to tell was one of sorrow and longing. She told me that she had fallen in love with a white man who came to our lands to talk of his Go—'

'That's my mother.' Jabuti cried out, interrupting her.

'I know Jabuti, I know,' she said with a warm smile playing upon her lips. 'She told me that she was made to leave the village by the elders who thought that she had brought shame upon them. Your shaman bitterly opposed them and fought for her to stay in the village but he was outvoted.'

'He told me that she was dead,' Jabuti said, feeling sadness and confusion that he had been so dreadfully deceived.

'He probably did it to save you from any more heartbreak Jabuti. Who would ever know that you would find yourself so far away from home and stumble upon the truth.

'So one terrible day she was led blindfolded and screaming from your village by several warriors who took her deep into the heart of the forest. After many days walk they released her with orders to never return. There was no chance that she would ever find her way back as she had never been more than half a day's walk from your village. So there she stood, alone, scared and mourning the loss of you, her son.'

Unable to control his emotions any longer Jabuti broke down completely, sobbing so hard that his body ached and he felt overwhelmed, fearing that he would lose his mind. With a silent look from Nakwatcha to the assembled gathering they arose silently from the fireside, leaving Jabuti with his friends and Samampo.

Jabuti slowly began to pull himself back together, taking deep cleansing breaths from the pit of his stomach. Looking around he was surprised to notice that the crowd had thinned to the remaining company.

'How do you feel?' Mapi asked.

'I feel better thank you Mapi, it came as such a shock after all this time to find out she is still alive,' Jabuti replied. 'Wait!' he cried out. 'If she is still alive then where is she?'

'Oh Jabuti, I hate to cause you more heartbreak but I don't know where she is now.'

'What do you mean you don't know?' Jabuti asked, feeling his longed for dreams being dashed, even before they had time to become a reality.

'After staying with us for many moons she became restless and finally left one morning, never to return.'

'Why did she leave?' Jabuti asked.

'She left in search of your father Jabuti. She knew she could never return to your village, let alone find it on her own, so she talked about heading downstream to where he had come from. She hoped that once he knew about you that he would lead her back to your village and she could hold you in her arms once again.'

'How she suffered,' Jabuti said, gazing off into the distance.

'You both have Jabuti, you both have.'

With that they left the three friends alone by the fire side.

'What are you thinking Jabuti?' Wanadi asked tentatively.

'Oh Wanadi I don't know. My head is swimming, my heart is racing, I don't know what to think,' he said in exasperation. 'From being an orphan I have found out that my father is a white man who may or may not be alive, and the same for my mother. I'm exhausted Wanadi, that's all I can say.'

'You need sleep Jabuti, it's more than just one man can cope with. Come let us take you to rest,' Wanadi said, leading him by the shoulders to their hut.

Making sure that he was comfortable, Wanadi and Mapi returned to the fireside to give their friend some space.

'Well Mapi, what do you make of that?'

'It's incredible Wanadi.'

'Let us hope that she is still alive. It's even more important that we reach our destination now.'

'So what do we do now?' Mapi asked.

'Well it's up to Jabuti, we'll leave when he's ready. But I must admit I quite like the idea of staying here for a while,' he replied, smiling at Mapi.

'I know what you mean Wanadi, but I still can't understand why there are no men here.'

'Who cares Mapi? They mean us no harm, besides who needs any competition with such beauties around.'

As if on cue Kachiri and Tatuie emerged out of the gloom to sit with the two friends by the fireside.

'What were you two talking about?' Kachiri asked.

'Oh nothing,' Mapi answered, almost too quickly.

'We were just talking about Jabuti and his mother,' Wanadi said, stepping in to save his friend's blushes. 'Did you know her?'

'Not really, I was a young child when she left,' she replied. 'Will you be staying with us for long?'

'Well we can't stay here forever, so we'll have to be leaving soon,' Wanadi replied.

'Not too soon I hope,' she said, looking up at him and held his gaze until he had to look away, feeling the colour rise up his neck.

'Oh, erm well we'll have to see what Jabuti thinks, you see h—'

'Wanadi, you're safe in our hands,' she said, interrupting him.

'Your friend is very quiet,' Mapi observed.

'Tatuie doesn't say much but she did tell me that she likes you Mapi.'

'Oh does she? Erm, well I like her too,' he said looking over at her, giving her an embarrassed smile.

The two friends sat feeling a little nervous not knowing what to do as they had never before found themselves in such a situation.

'I suppose we'd better get some sleep,' Wanadi finally said, breaking the silence.

'And disturb your friend, don't you think he needs some peace and quiet?' Kachiri asked.

'Hmm, yes I suppose you're right,' Wanadi said, sitting down again. 'We can stay for a little bit longer, what do you say Mapi?'

'Oh yes, yes please,' he replied, looking over at Tatuie, his earlier feelings of embarrassment seemingly vanished.

'Great!' Kachiri said. 'How about a drink?' she asked as she pulled a container from the shadows and poured a drink for each of them.

Feeling more relaxed Wanadi gladly accepted as he drunk heartily from it, immediately gasping at the strength of it. Looking over at Mapi he saw his eyes bulge as he took a sip.

'Do you like it?' Kachiri asked.

'It's strong,' Wanadi replied. 'Much like the Sar that we make in our village, what is in it?'

'I don't know,' she replied. 'Only a handful of the older women know the ingredients, and they keep it a secret, I don't think they trust us,' she said, giggling along with Tatuie.

'So why are there no men here?' Mapi asked, feeling emboldened by the fortifying drink and the pleasant company.

'Mapi!' Wanadi scolded.

'It's alright Mapi,' Kachiri replied. 'We have no need of men, we can do everything a man can, and it leads to a more peaceful life.'

'I knew it,' Mapi said.

Wanadi smiled at him but nearly choked at Mapi's next comment.

'Well you can't do everything that a man can, can you?'

Silence ensued as Mapi shrank inwards fearing that he had overstepped the mark. Wanadi looked over at him in alarm with his cup half raised to his lips.

'Oh, Mapi,' Tatuie finally said, breaking her silence and started giggling. 'Can't do everything a man can,' she repeated. 'Ooh Mapi, you're so funny.'

The two friends raised their eyebrows at each other in surprise, but couldn't help but join in with the laughter. Soon they were chatting amiably, swapping stories and the reasons for their journey with Jabuti. Determined not to drink too much like he had done too many times recently Wanadi suggested that it was time for bed, but he was left feeling dumbstruck when Kachiri arose and led him by the hand towards her sleeping quarters. Sneaking a quick peek over his shoulder towards Mapi he raised his eyebrows in surprise to see him looking startled.

'Oh well, I suppose I'd better ge—' Mapi began.

'Shh, Mapi,' Tatuie said as she led him by the hand away from the fireside.

CHAPTER SIXTEEN

Meanwhile Jabuti had fallen asleep as soon as he laid his head upon the straw matting and began dreaming vividly of his mother. He found himself walking down a forest path so dark that he could hardly see his hand in front of his face, as he experienced a sense of panic. Stumbling along the gloomy path he felt a presence calling out to him from the inky blackness. Even though he couldn't make out what the voice was saying he drew comfort from it, feeling drawn to it as it held an air of familiarity in its warm notes. Drawing closer he finally made out the words that were calling out to him enticingly.

'Jabuti, Jabuti,' the enigmatic voice whispered.

'Who's there?' he called out, but the voice continued calling out his name, not caring that he was stumbling around blindly in the darkness. 'Mother, is that you?' he cried out in desperation.

'Jabuti, Jabuti,' came the haunting refrain again.

'Mother, is it really you?'

'Jabuti, it's Samampo, shh now.'

'No... what... where are you mother?' he moaned, thrashing about in his half dreaming state.

'Jabuti, wake up it's me Samampo.'

'Samampo, what are you doing here?' he asked in shock as he was brought back into the real world. 'I was dreaming of my mother,' he told her, devastated that it was but a dream.

'I know Jabuti, I came to see if you needed anything and I saw you sleeping restlessly so I decided to stay.'

'Thank you, where are Wanadi and Mapi?'

'They're alright, they're with Kachiri and Tatuie. They thought you might need some time alone.'

'I see, well thank you for your kindness.'

'It must have been quite a shock to find out about your mother.'

'Yes it was, I don't know what to feel. I can't even begin to hope that she is still alive, I couldn't cope with any more disappointment in my life,' he replied, feeling awkward that he had shared too much with a woman he hardly knew.

'I admire you Jabuti for your strength, I don't know what I would do if I lost my mother.'

Feeling vulnerable he began to cry unashamedly in front of her. As he did so she leant forward taking his head in her hands and rested it upon her shoulders.

'Shh, Jabuti, shh,' she gently cooed into his ear and brushed his hair with her hand.

Sniffing back the tears he looked up into her kind green eyes, feeling drawn towards her as their lips gently brushed each other. Immediately he felt the same excitement that he had when he first kissed Maru. What am I doing? he suddenly thought. At that instant he abruptly pulled back from her warm embrace

'I can't do this.'

'Do what Jabuti? We're only kissing,' she said in her mischievous way.

'I know, but I have someone back home waiting for me. I asked her to wait for me, I couldn't live with myself or ever look into her eyes honestly if I carried on with this; I'm sorry.'

'She won't know,' she said, leaning into him once more.

'No Samampo, I can't,' he told her, pushing her away with more force than he meant to as she fell sprawling onto the floor in front of him.

'Samampo, I'm sorry, I don't know what came over me.'

'Men!' she spat out with menace and such a look of venom in her eyes that it sent a shiver running through his bones. With that one word she brushed herself down, never once taking her eyes off him and departed into the gloom of the night.

Several hours passed as he tossed and turned, unable to switch off all the thoughts that were whirling around in his mind. Eventually he drifted off into sleep with strange, unconnected and vivid dreams entering his mind uninvited. He awoke, feeling heavy-headed and tired from his restless sleep and peered out from the doorway. Worryingly he sensed a strange atmosphere as he spied a huddle of women who looked his way with a collective harsh stare. Feeling uncomfortable under their gaze he looked past them to see Wanadi and Mapi walking his way with shoulders slumped and their gaze averted to the path. Sensing something seriously wrong he walked cautiously towards his friends.

'What's wrong Wanadi?'

'We have to leave Jabuti.'

'What do you mean we have to leave?'

'There's no time to explain we ha—'

'You heard him Jabuti, it's time for you to go,' Samampo interrupted Wanadi, as she walked up behind him.

'I don't understand, I'm sorry for what happened last night. I wanted to explain to you this morning,' Jabuti replied, noticing that all of the women of the village stood behind Samampo in solidarity.

Jabuti felt chilled as to how a look of warmth and friendship had so quickly been replaced by one of open hostility.

'Jabuti, you are just a man, you would never understand. But alas, you men have something that we do not, but your friends willingly provided us with that last night,' she said, looking towards them with a sneer and a look of contempt on her face.

With the eyes of the whole village bearing down on them with undisguised hatred, Wanadi and Mapi continued staring at the ground.

'Leave, we have what we need now.' The women pressed forward and it wasn't until that point that Jabuti noticed that they were armed with spears and bows and arrows.

'Get your belongings now and never return.'

Visibly shaken and confused the three friends rushed towards their hut and quickly grabbed their packs and returned to the threatening atmosphere. Jabuti opened his mouth to say something but decided better of it and they reluctantly turned to depart on the forest path on which they had arrived.

'Oh, Jabuti,' Samampo called out to him, 'if you hadn't been so much of a boy last night then you could have walked away like a man.'

Jabuti felt the pain of humiliation as they walked away with the sound of the women's laughter and mocking accompanying them.

CHAPTER SEVENTEEN

They walked for a while in silence, shocked and dismayed at their recent reversal of fortunes. One moment they were comfortable in the surroundings and warmth of a friendly society, the next they were ousted in the most brutal of manners; just as they were beginning to recuperate. They continued walking along the riverbank for a while until they were certain they were a safe distance away from the village and sat down.

'What just happened back there?' Mapi asked, bewildered at what had just transpired.

'They used us Mapi,' Wanadi replied.

'What do you mean?'

'Mapi, come on, you're not that innocent. Remember what happened last night?'

'Yes, but what…?' Mapi began. 'Oh I see, do you mean th—'

'Yes Mapi,' interrupted Wanadi, 'they used us like animals. That is how they continue their race.'

'But I don't understand why they would want to live like that, without men. Where were all the little boys then?'

'I don't think we really want to think about that Mapi,' Wanadi replied, grim faced. 'I think we had a lucky escape.'

Jabuti looked at them confused until Wanadi told him what had transpired the previous evening.

'What happened to you last night?' Wanadi asked.

Jabuti told them of his encounter with Samampo and his feelings of guilt that it was he who had caused the sudden change in atmosphere.

'No Jabuti, don't feel guilty,' Wanadi said. 'If you had given in then we would all have been used, then how could you have ever have looked into Maru's eyes again?'

'Thank you Wanadi,' Jabuti replied. 'I saw such anger in Samampo's eyes that it chilled me to the bone. I don't even want to think about the evil that they're capable of.'

They sat in silence for a while, reflecting on their unusual and chilling encounter.

'It was good though,' Wanadi said after a while and nudging Mapi in the process. His attempt at humour lightened the atmosphere as they began chatting amongst themselves.

'So, what now Jabuti?' Mapi asked.

'Well Mapi, my faithful friend, we continue downriver if you're still with me?'

'I'm with you Jabuti, even more so now we know your mother may be still alive.'

'Yes Jabuti, me too,' Wanadi said. 'That is one good thing that came out of our recent experience, oh and now Mapi finally knows what it is like to be with a woman.'

'I heard you Wanadi, crying like a little girl as she kissed you.' Mapi teased back.

Continuing on their journey Jabuti began to think more and more of the danger he had put his friends in and realised the futility of their situation. Slowly his mood transformed into a dark and somber one as doubts continued to flood his mind. How could my mother still be alive, how will I ever find my father, how stupid must I be? he thought.

'Paah!' he spat out in frustration, kicking the dry earth in front of him.

'Hey, hey Jabuti what's wrong?!' Wanadi asked, surprised at Jabuti's reversal in mood.

'It's nothing, forget it,' he snapped.

'We're in this together Jabuti, come on tell us,' Mapi said.

'I'm sorry, it's just that … I don't know what to think,' he replied. 'Bah! Why me?' he shouted out to the tree tops and sank to his knees in frustration.

Wanadi and Mapi rushed to his side offering kind words and exchanged concerned looks for the destitute state of their friend.

'What is it Jabuti?' Mapi asked, looking into his friend's eyes.

Jabuti sat on the forest floor looking like a dejected child and after a while he began to speak, 'How can I explain a lifetime of longing and heartache, how can I let you know the pain I have suffered watching you grow up, with the comfort of your mothers' warm embrace and your fathers' guidance? Oh, I know your parents treated me like one of their own,' he said, looking towards his two friends. 'But I always felt like an outsider looking in, yearning for a family of my own.

'Now everything I have longed for has suddenly become possible and within my reach. It feels so real that I can almost sense it, but what if I never find them, what if they no longer want to see me, what if they are de…?' he trailed off as Wanadi and Mapi leaned forward to comfort him.

'Jabuti, you are trying and that's all that matters. You are the strongest man I know, I can't even imagine the suffering you've been through. Mapi and I are here for you in whatever you choose to do,' he said as Mapi nodded in agreement. 'If you want to turn back that's fine, if you want to continue then that's fine also.'

Jabuti sat in silence, absorbing the kind words of his friends, 'Can we continue?' he said eventually.

'That's what I was hoping you'd say,' Wanadi replied.

Putting many days and nights behind them they continued downriver on their journey. Jabuti began to feel lighter in spirit, sensing all the trials and tribulations of the recent past beginning to ebb away. Still, he felt nervous as he sensed they were nearing their destination and then he would have to prepare himself for whatever might happen. Along their journey they slowly begun to notice a change in their surroundings, with various streams and canals leading off from the main river, widening as it did so.

The trees changed shape indiscernibly from massive structures to smaller, squat creations with roots and branches sticking out in every direction. With the water tasting brackish they had to conserve what little they had with them and search for rain water collected in plants and hollows of branches. The solid ground which had aided them so well on their journey soon changed as their feet were sucked into foul, stinking mud with every step. Their torture continued for several days with the friends becoming weaker and weaker all the time and a raging thirst adding to their problems.

With the river widening more and more they had no choice but to keep to its margins, for to negotiate a way inland through the tangle of roots and branches was virtually impossible. Much to their relief and with their energy waning they spotted a sandy shelf in the distance which seemed to stretch for as far as the eye could see. But for them, time stretched into an eternity as the cloying, putrefying mud refused to let go, as if sensing their desperation to escape its clutches. With bellies aching from hunger, mouths dry and lips scabbed over from lack of water they managed to drag their exhausted bodies through the mud and haul themselves onto the sand. They lay panting and groaning after days of continual hardship and deprivation and immediately fell asleep.

'Look at the state of you two,' Jabuti said after waking, noticing their pitiful condition.

'Have you seen yourself, you don't look much better?' Mapi answered, smiling at his friend.

'Come on then, let's have a wash,' Jabuti said, walking to the edge of the water.

'Do you think there'll be some half naked women watching us?' Wanadi joked with a glint in his eye.

'I think we've had enough excitement for a life time,' Jabuti replied with a grin.

Enjoying the feeling of washing all the mud and vegetation off their weary bodies they sat in the shallows afterwards, splashing each other with water.

'Why does this water taste so bitter Jabuti?' Mapi asked, spitting it out.

'I don't know Mapi, but we are far from home, things are different here.' Jabuti replied.

'Do you think we're close to the white men's village?'

'Well the shaman said that they came from across the water that never ends. It looks big enough to me, I can't see across to the other side,' he said, indicating the wide expanse of the estuary as it opened up into the sea.

'So Jabuti, what do you want do now?' Wanadi asked.

'Well, first of all we have to search inland for fresh water if we can and fill our skins up.'

'And get some food,' Mapi said with a hungry look.

'Yes Mapi, food as well.'

The deeper they ventured into the forest the more they noticed the vegetation returning a little to what they were more used to back at home. No longer did they have to negotiate the fortress of sharp roots sticking through the mud, waiting to catch them out at every turn. Trekking through the forest they came across many unusual animals of a kind they had never encountered before. They saw giant sea otters floating on their backs, eating freshly caught piranha held firmly in their paws as they kept a wary eye on the armoured crocodiles drifting past them with a menacing aura. The friends were truly frightened by the sight of the crocodiles for they were much larger than the caimans they knew back home. They could quite happily swim amongst the caimans back at their village unconcerned for their safety, but just one look at their monstrous bodies told them that it would not be a good idea. Looking at them warily they were startled by the noise of river dolphins exhaling air through their blowholes as they came up to breathe.

This truly is a land much different to ours Jabuti thought, gazing around in wonderment at his surroundings. Further upstream the water tasted less bitter as they carefully filled up their skins, ever watchful for the crocodiles that skimmed the surface with just their eyes and snouts showing. They sat down against the base of a large tree and gulped the fresh tasting water down greedily, and washed the salty water from their bodies. Feeling relaxed and with their thirst sated they became aware of a sound of snorting and a strange type of whistling of the kind they had never heard before. Looking around the base of the trunk they laid eyes upon a tapir, with its mane of hair and extended snout, rustling and snorting about in the forest litter.

'What is that?' Mapi whispered.

'Food,' Wanadi said.

With an unspoken agreement and with complete silence on Wanadi's part he slowly got to his knees and drew back his bow, sending it swiftly on its deathly course deep into the animal's heart. With just a short snuffling sound it sank to its knees, dying quickly. So hungry were they after their arduous journey that they immediately began preparing its carcass to eat. After lighting a fire and tasting of its flesh they decided that it was similar to the meat of the pig that they were more used to. With their bellies full they felt re-energised and ready to continue on their journey; wherever it took them.

Making sure that they filled their skins up to the brim and cutting up the tastiest morsels of their kill they made to leave. They decided that they would return to the coast in the hope that they might find the white men's village there. Just as they were packing up to leave and from nowhere a huge black jaguar pounced into the heart of their makeshift camp sending them ducking for cover. Grunting and growling it sat low on its haunches and eyed them up with a cautious, yet hungry look.

'Don't move Mapi,' Wanadi barked as he saw him preparing to run.

'Mapi, listen to him,' Jabuti snapped.

'Bu—' Mapi began.

'Keep quiet,' Wanadi whispered.

Wanadi eyed his spear which was lying propped up against the tree in readiness for their departure. Unfortunately it was out of his reach as he kept one eye on the snarling animal. Sensing Mapi's fright and weakness the animal turned towards him and started inching its way forwards when Mapi turned to flee.

'No Mapi, no!' Wanadi shouted at him.

Alerted and distracted by Wanadi's scream the animal pounced towards him as fast as lightning, swiping at his torso with its razor-sharp claws. Equally fast was Jabuti who grabbed his spear and thrust it deep into the animal's neck and it fell to the ground with a final grunt.

'Wanadi!' they both screamed, rushing to his side as he lay bleeding from several terrible, deep gashes.

'I'm sorry.' Mapi said, concern etched into his features.

'You never did listen to me,' he managed to croak through a thin smile.

'Mapi, Mapi!' Jabuti shouted out to him, snapping him out of his shock.

'Stay with Wanadi whilst I find something to help the bleeding.'

Jabuti ran to the edge of the river and grabbed clumps of moss which were known to him to hold antiseptic properties and could soak up blood loss in emergencies. To Jabuti's eyes the moss looked no different to the ones that grew back home so he rushed to Wanadi's side and gently packed it in and around his wound. As Jabuti would have expected of Wanadi's bravery he flinched only ever so slightly.

'What shall we do Jabuti?'

With Wanadi slipping into unconsciousness Jabuti became truly worried, but he didn't want to show it for fear of scaring Mapi.

'We need to find help straight away,' Jabuti replied, as he looked at the blood oozing from Wanadi's injury.

'From where?' Mapi asked, stretching his arms to indicate the wilderness they found themselves in.

'I don't know Mapi,' Jabuti snapped at him. 'I don't know,' he repeated more kindly, then whispered to him, 'I fear that Wanadi might not survive if we don't find help.'

'Maybe we can find some honey to help him Jabuti,' Mapi said in desperation, referring to the healing properties it held.

'That's a good idea Mapi but we don't know this area, it could take us days to find a bee's nest,' Jabuti replied. 'No, we just have to keep moving. If we see any along the way then we shall stop. But I fear his injury will need more than just honey.'

Jabuti looked across at his friend who looked distraught.

'It wasn't your fault Mapi.'

'But…'

'Come on Mapi, you have to act strong for Wanadi. We need to move him, we must be near to the village by now,' he told him.

Jabuti harboured doubts that they were close but he couldn't share his concerns with Mapi. The village could be within a day's walk or even further he thought. All he knew was that he would walk day and night to save his friend's life. Looking down at Wanadi's angry and bloodied wound he thought about treating it the same as he done with Mapi, but such was the depth and size he thought he might do more damage than good. To take Mapi's mind off Wanadi's predicament he set him the task of finding materials to build a stretcher. Whilst Mapi was busy searching for the supplies Jabuti knelt down by his friend's side, holding his hand as he did so.

'Wanadi, look at what has happened to you through my selfish desires,' Jabuti said, becoming really angry as he looked down at the wrecked body of his friend. 'Oh spirits of the forest why do you keep testing me, look at my friend who suffers, is it not enough that you have put so much in our path to test our courage?'

Feeling the anger welling up inside of him and with unbridled passion he continued, 'And what of the white men's God, who is so powerful that men leave their own lands to spread their word here. Where are you to be seen, what help are you? And what use have these lucky charms been?' he shouted out and wrenched the small leather pouch from his loin-cloth that the shaman had given him. He threw it away into the forest and sunk to his knees in frustration.

By now Mapi had returned and stood open-mouthed as he watched Jabuti shouting out in anger, 'Jabuti, Jabuti,' Mapi called out to him, with his arms full of wood and palm fronds.

Jabuti turned towards him with a hollow and defeated look and seemed to gaze right through him as if he wasn't there. Mapi walked up to him and bent down to look him in the eyes, 'Jabuti, we will get through this,' he said, smiling at him. He walked to where Jabuti had thrown the pouch and returned it hesitantly to him. 'Here, this was a gift Jabuti, take it.'

'Thank you Mapi.' Jabuti said.

They both sat in silence as Jabuti took deep breaths to cleanse his mind and he slowly calmed down. Looking at the returned pouch Jabuti held it in his hands and jumped up exclaiming, 'Mapi, I completely forgot!'

'Forgot what?'

'The shaman, he gave me this,' Jabuti said, opening the pouch and showed Mapi the shavings of the capi vine which still remained safe inside. 'He said it would give me strength, maybe we can give some to Wanadi; it might help him.'

'It's worth a try Jabuti,' Mapi answered in eagerness.

Jabuti knelt over Wanadi and opened his mouth gently and placed a wad of it inside of his cheek and sat back, hoping for the best.

With nothing more that could be done for Wanadi they set about the task of constructing a stretcher. When completed they gently lifted Wanadi onto it and began retracing their steps. After walking for several hours the strain began to tell with the weight of carrying their stricken friend. With shoulders and arms aching and with sweat pouring from their brows neither wanted to look weak in front of the other by giving in. So they continued plodding forward, ignoring their wracked bodies screaming out in pain.

Just when Mapi thought he could take no more Jabuti called for them to rest.

'We'll be no good to Wanadi if we exhaust ourselves.'

'Maybe we can use some of the capi vine Jabuti, I don't think I can go on much further.'

'Why not Mapi, the shaman gave it to me for a purpose.'

Jabuti opened up the pouch and shared the last of the shavings between them and they sat chewing it. Almost immediately Jabuti felt a rush of energy surge through his body and his fingers started to tingle. He felt his body lighten as all his muscular aches and pains seemed to vanish.

'The shaman was right Mapi, how do you feel?'

'Like I could walk for days.'

'Come on then,' Jabuti said as they picked up the stretcher and continued.

As they carried on walking Jabuti began to notice the colours of the forest in a vividness he hadn't been aware of before. The emerald-green of the foliage seemed to flash to Jabuti in various different hues and swayed in a kaleidoscopic breeze. The sounds of animals calling out to each other magnified in his head and seemed to be talking to him. Jabuti shook his head and concentrated on bearing the weight of his stricken friend and continued carrying the back of the stretcher.

Is that my father walking ahead of me, why is he turning his back to me when I've come so far to see him? he wondered. Jabuti tried calling out to him but his tongue felt heavy and his mouth refused to obey his commands. He thought that he would walk ahead of him and attract his attention but his arms felt heavy and pinned to his sides.

Abruptly his mind became alert once more and he looked towards Mapi but decided not to worry him with his experience and kept on walking.

Eventually they called a halt to rest as they felt the effects of the vine wearing off and laid down by the river. Jabuti closed his eyes just for a moment to rest his weary eyes. He soon found himself being awoken by Mapi who signalled him to be quiet with his fingers to pursed lips. Jabuti immediately sat up and looked towards Wanadi.

'He's alright Jabuti,' Mapi said, seeing the concerned look on his face. 'I've heard some voices coming from the river.'

He crept with Mapi towards the edge of the river, where they saw in the distance two men paddling a craft very similar in construction to their bongo. They stared incredulously as they paddled closer and closer to their location, landing virtually within arms-reach.

They watched the two men alight from their craft, enraptured by their appearance. They wore only a thin cord around their waists which was attached to the end of their penises, their faces and bodies were decorated in elaborate swirls of brown paint with fine sticks protruding from their noses, ears and chins. Jabuti listened intently to their speech and found that he couldn't understand a word of what was being said between them. The two men leaned into their craft after tying it up securely and pulled out some hunting gear and headed off into the forest. Watching them intently a thought entered Jabuti's mind, one which he wasn't comfortable with but he felt unavoidable nonetheless.

'I've had an idea Mapi.'

'I agree with you,' he answered.

'I haven't told you yet Mapi.'

'You want to take their bongo,' Mapi said with a look of understanding. 'I know you would do anything to help your friends, Jabuti.'

'It's just that I don't think Wanadi will survive.'

'I know Jabuti, you don't have to explain to me.'

Jabuti smiled at his friend.

'What kind of trouble are we going to get into this time?' Mapi asked with a wry grin.

CHAPTER EIGHTEEN

They spent time remaining where they were to be sure that the strange looking men were not going to return. Once they were sure they were safe Jabuti crept up to where the bongo pointed downstream, fighting against its tether. Aware of the recent incidents that they had encountered Jabuti was ever cautious and inched forwards. Expecting them to leap upon him from the forest at any time he quickly untied it, keeping a wary eye on the shadows. He hopped in and grabbed a paddle to make the short distance towards Mapi. Grounding the vessel he jumped onto the riverbank and wasting no time, he and Mapi lifted Wanadi into the bottom and they climbed in either end.

'Quick Mapi, before they come back,' Jabuti urged him.

Just as his words were uttered they heard a commotion coming from behind them. They turned to look and to their horror they saw the two tribesmen shouting and raising their bows to fire at them. Jabuti and Mapi ducked instinctively, hoping that the low sides of the bongo might offer some protection. Expecting arrows to be flying all around them they slowly raised their heads to see a look of resignation in the strangers' faces as they saw their craft disappearing. Jabuti who was in the front turned to look at Mapi and the instant their eyes met they burst into laughter at the relief of having escaped another dangerous situation.

Even though Wanadi lay gravely ill Jabuti knew that he would have joined in with the laughter too. They continued paddling to where the river met the water with no end and stopped to decide which way to turn.

'I think we should go this way,' Jabuti said, pointing to the right.

'Why?' Mapi asked.

'I don't know Mapi, it's either this way or that,' he replied, shrugging his shoulders.

'Come on then,' Mapi said and grabbing his paddle he pulled with his shoulders as it bit into the water. They paddled for the rest of the day and into the evening, ignoring the pain screaming out from their aching muscles. All the while they administered to Wanadi's wound and poured water into his mouth. Imperceptibly dawn began to break as they continued on their weary trek, passing river mouths both big and small. Just when Mapi was nearing the end of his endurance he spotted smoke rising up from within the forest, along one of the tributaries.

'Jabuti, look,' he said, pointing towards it and Jabuti followed with lazy, tired eyes.

'Well done Mapi, I would have missed that,' he replied, suddenly alert.

'What shall we do?'

'Let's go and have a look.'

Hugging the riverbank they paddled upstream and pulled the bongo deep into the forest, covering it with palm fronds and branches to help camouflage it into its surroundings. Mapi stayed with Wanadi to administer to him and Jabuti crept off a short distance, crouching low as he tuned into his surroundings. Hearing no voices or anything suspicious he stood up and moved forward with the smell of the smoke to guide him. After several minutes he arrived into a clearing and the sight that greeted him made him gasp.

In front of him were two tall wooden crosses and a central courtyard with several simply constructed buildings running alongside. As his eyes took in the unfamiliar structures his eyes were led towards a large and imposing edifice which lay at the heart of the settlement. The building had walls of dried mud and a peaked roof of dried palm leaves with a simple wooden cross placed on top. Leading down from the roof were exquisitely carved and painted wooden pillars, with gold painted diamonds and flowers. Set in the middle were two large intricately designed wooden doors, keeping whatever lay inside secret from his inquisitive eyes. Whoever had built the fire was nowhere to be seen, so he decided to walk back to confer with Mapi. Upon arrival he breathlessly told Mapi of all that he had seen and he listened in awe at his description.

'What shall we do?' Mapi asked.

'I don't think we have any choice Mapi, look at Wanadi,' he said, indicating his friend who was looking pale and hardly breathing.

They arrived in the courtyard carrying Wanadi between them and laid him down carefully on the bare earth as Jabuti cried out for help. Several moments elapsed with no reaction, then the doors of the large building opened and out stepped a white man. He was dressed in a simple costume of a long grey tunic buttoned at the neck with a crisp, white collar protruding and a grey-coloured skull cap. His tunic was fastened around the middle by a simple leather belt and he stood barefooted in front of them.

He was a tall man with a weather beaten face and kind eyes, with lines etched around them which exuded an aura of calm and wisdom to Jabuti. He had a thick mane of white hair and a white beard and Jabuti stood mesmerised looking at his imposing features. Noticing Wanadi's bloodied body the man rushed towards him with a look of genuine concern and started to examine his wounds in an expert manner.

Looking up at Jabuti he spoke to him in tongues that he had never heard before and Jabuti looked at him in confusion until the man asked, 'What has happened my child?'

'He has been attacked by a jaguar.'

'Let me look,' the man said. 'I can help, you can let go of him,' he said softly, with a comforting smile. He shouted out in another language to inquisitive faces which Jabuti noticed peering out from the open doorways. Both friends looked on in concern as two tribesmen dressed in white costumes rushed to Wanadi's side and carried him effortlessly away.

'Do not worry, he is sick but I can help. Wait here, I will return,' the white man said.

'Please be careful with him, he is a very good friend,' Jabuti said as he stood up, concerned for Wanadi's welfare.

The man put a comforting hand on his shoulder and said, 'I have medicine, rest here, you are safe with us.'

He did as instructed and watched them carry Wanadi away. Afterwards Jabuti and Mapi sat on the bare earth in a companionable silence, exhausted by their recent travails.

Jabuti then noticed that several more people dressed in immaculate white clothing were walking towards them. He nudged Mapi and they watched them approach with kindly smiles upon their faces. They knelt down in front of Jabuti and Mapi with plates of freshly cut fruit and tender morsels of meat.

They spoke to them in several languages that Jabuti could not understand and when he shrugged they motioned for him and Mapi to eat from the plates.

Whilst they were eating, several women tended carefully to the cuts and scrapes they had suffered from walking through the forest. When they had their fill the same women washed them down with scented water and Jabuti felt a sense of wellbeing as they selflessly cared for him and Mapi.

They were then led to one of the buildings that lined the courtyard where they were offered to rest. Jabuti noticed with interest that they slept not upon the floor but on beds made of wooden frames and woven matting. Their hosts motioned for them to lie on the beds and gracefully exited, leaving them alone.

'Well Mapi what do you...?' Jabuti asked, turning towards his friend but stopped himself as he saw him sleeping soundly. Jabuti smiled and soon afterwards he drifted into a deep sleep as well.

They awoke to find the kindly man with white hair looking down upon them with his hands clasped in front of him.

'How is Wanadi?' Jabuti asked immediately, sensing that he might have come to tell them something dreadful.

'Your friend?' he said. 'Do not worry, he sleeps. I have cleaned and dressed his wound and he suffers less.'

'Thank you,' Jabuti said, breathing a sigh of relief.

'What are your names?' the man asked.

'I am Jabuti and he is Mapi,' Jabuti replied and Mapi then awoke to the sounds of their conversation.

'What is your name?'

'I go by the name of Rodrigo,' he replied.

'Are you a man of God?' Jabuti asked.

'Yes my child,' he replied with a smile. 'What brings you to our village?'

At that question Jabuti and Mapi shared a look and laughed as the sense of relief washed over them. Rodrigo stood and watched with a patient and amused look on his face as the two of them began to compose themselves once more.

'I'm sorry Rodrigo,' Jabuti said. 'It's just that we have come a long way to find your village, and we have suffered so much along the way. I just thought this day would never come.'

'Tell me all about it Jabuti,' Rodrigo said with interest. Mapi took that as his cue to leave them alone and he left them to wander around their new surroundings. Jabuti sat up, took a deep breath and began to tell him everything. He told him of the village where they came from, his feelings of loneliness, his meeting with the shaman and their journey through the forest and of their meeting with the white men. At his news Rodrigo suddenly stopped Jabuti in mid-flow.

'You say this man of God went by the name of Alonso?'

'Yes, did you know him?'

'Yes Jabuti, he is one of my most dedicated brothers. I thought that he had died in the forest; he has been gone a long time now.'

'I'm afraid he is dead Rodrigo, he died saving our lives,' Jabuti informed him.

'Oh my, he always was a very brave man. Tell me what happened, Jabuti.'

The story took several hours and throughout it all Rodrigo's eyes never faltered as he gazed at Jabuti, enthralled by his tale. Jabuti finished by asking him if he knew of his father Pedro.

'Yes indeed I do know him,' he replied with a look of concern. 'I am upset to hear of his relationship with your mother, it isn't what God has taught us to do. I'm sorry Jabuti.'

'It's fine, I have had time to think about it, if it wasn't for him then I wouldn't be here,' Jabuti said with a smile. 'What can you tell me about him, is he still here, is he in the forest preaching of your God?' Jabuti asked in eagerness.

'Oh Jabuti I'm so sorry, you have come all this way only for me to give you bad news.' Jabuti felt his body stiffen as he prepared himself for what was coming. 'He left to return to our country many moons ago; he was very ill.'

Jabuti sat in the darkened atmosphere of the room, feeling stunned by Rodrigo's revelation and he felt his head swim as the walls seemed to close in around him. He suddenly leapt up from the bed and ran out into the courtyard and fell to his knees gasping for breath as Mapi appeared and ran to his aid.

'What's wrong Jabuti?'

'My father's not here Mapi, he's gone!'

'Oh Jabuti,' Mapi said with compassion and hugged him tightly.

Rodrigo appeared out of the gloom and stepped into the courtyard.

'What kind of God would do this to just one person, have I not suffered enough?' Jabuti shouted to him. 'Answer me that.'

'I know it is hard for you to understand right now. I can't begin to tell you God's reasons, but he is loving and kind.'

'I want no part of a God like that,' Jabuti said as he sat on his haunches and stared at Rodrigo.

'I think we need time alone please,' Mapi said.

'I understand, I shall be in our house of worship if you wish to join me later,' he said, walking towards the church.

'Oh Jabuti, I'm so sorry for you.'

'I feel foolish, I've dragged you so far and for nothing.'

'It wasn't for nothing Jabuti, your mother could still be alive,' Mapi said kindly.

'How?' he snapped back. 'How could that be possible after all these years?'

'You never know, sh—'

'I do know Mapi,' Jabuti said, interrupting him. 'I just know,' he said with finality.

'So, what now Jabuti?'

'I will go and talk with Rodrigo in his house of worship.'

With that he left Mapi and walked towards the majestic building, whereupon he marvelled at the intricate carvings on the door as he steeled himself to enter. Upon entering he took in the sight of neatly laid out wooden pews which led towards a raised altar. He stood enthralled and gazed in wonder at various objects which seemed to be made of the same material as the *oro* that they had brought along with them.

Jabuti saw Rodrigo in front of the altar kneeling down with his head bowed and his hands held in front of him. Jabuti stood silently not wishing to disturb him and his eyes rested upon a carving of a man on a wooden cross similar to the ones in the courtyard. Jabuti was shocked to see an image like that in a place of worship as he looked at the blood which was painted on his hands and feet. What was such a haunting figure doing here? he mused. As if sensing his presence and perhaps his unease Rodrigo turned to see Jabuti standing in the shadows and asked him to join him.

'I'm glad you came,' he said as he arose to greet him. 'How are you feeling?'

'I don't know Rodrigo, I have come so far only to face disappointment once more.'

'I can't even begin to imagine how you are feeling.'

'Only time will tell, I feel stupid and reckless for bringing my friends on this wasted journey. How can I ever face everyone back at my village now?'

'It wasn't a wasted journey Jabuti, your father is still alive, you know where he is now.'

'But what use is that to me now that he has travelled back across the water with no end?'

'It does have an end Jabuti, it ends in our land which we call *España.*'

'*Es-pa-ña?*' he repeated. 'I wish to learn your language as well as you speak mine.'

'I was a teacher of languages in my country. I have lived here a long time, I speak the tongues of many tribes.'

'Tell me of your land Rodrigo.'

They moved to one of the simple wooden pews and sat down, whereupon Rodrigo told him of his country and his reasons for coming to Jabuti's land. He told him that back home he was an educated man who taught in a large building where people would come to hear him speak. He said that he felt a sense of unease with the life he was living and had a need to search for something more meaningful in his life. Jabuti smiled upon hearing that, for it held a resonance with the journey he had just undertaken.

Rodrigo told him of his decision to join a group of God-fearing people called the Jesuits who travelled to different lands to spread his word. Their work was arduous and dangerous and many of Rodrigo's friends had died in the pursuit of their beliefs; either through illness or being killed by hostile tribes. Jabuti admired the bravery of the man who sat beside him, who had risked all of that for a God whom he could not see or hear. For Jabuti, who came from a society where they did not believe in such things it felt strange to him, but he respected him nonetheless.

Rodrigo tried to tell him of other lands called Japan and Europe where many of his fellow believers resided and taught but it was too much for Jabuti to comprehend. Many hours passed as they talked, and through the process Jabuti felt himself becoming less bitter and angry when he spoke with Rodrigo.

'Come with me Jabuti, I have something to show you,' Rodrigo said afterwards, with sadness in his eyes.

Jabuti followed him outside, wondering what it could be. He walked with Rodrigo towards the back of the church and through into a well-manicured garden with flowers and an immaculate path running through it. Jabuti was confused to see numerous small crosses dotted within the confines of the garden, painted a brilliant white.

'What is this place?' Jabuti asked, wondering why Rodrigo had brought him to see a garden of crosses.

'It is what we call a *cementerio,*' Rodrigo replied.

'I don't understand.'

'This is where we bury our dead.'

Jabuti nodded respectfully and asked, 'But why have you brought me here?'

'Come,' he said softly and led him a short way up the path and stopped in front of one of the simple white crosses.

Jabuti looked at him in confusion as he felt a sudden wave of nausea wash over him.

'This is where your mother Pucu lays.'

'No!' Jabuti screamed as he fell in a heap at Rodrigo's feet, 'No!'

CHAPTER NINETEEN

The next few days were difficult for Jabuti as he tried to come to terms with the death of his mother; all over again. Rodrigo told him of the day his mother had arrived into the village, half-starved and delirious. She had been found by a local fishing tribe who knew of Rodrigo's village and took her there to be healed. Unfortunately she never recovered fully, even with Rodrigo's tender care. She did tell him however, in between fits of unconsciousness, her extraordinary story of hardship and deprivation.

Rodrigo knew Jabuti was Pucu's son the moment he began to tell his story but he wanted to wait for the right moment to tell him of her passing. Jabuti spent his days wandering around the peaceful settlement in a daze, either sitting by the grave of his dear departed mother, or within the peaceful confines of the church. With Wanadi still gravely ill, Mapi proved to be a pillar of strength for Jabuti as he was there when he needed to talk, and he gave him space when he needed to be alone. Mapi spent that time by Wanadi's bedside, administering to him and telling him everything that had been going on.

Meanwhile Jabuti would join Rodrigo within the church, where they spoke of matters of religion and the world beyond the confines of their settlement.

Several times Jabuti raged against the injustice of it all and cried tears and felt emotions he was never aware he held deep within him. Throughout it all Rodrigo took all of Jabuti's rage, never showing any emotion, even when Jabuti questioned the integrity of the God in which Rodrigo believed. Jabuti gained strength though from the white man, with his calm nature and unshakeable belief in his calling.

He learned more of his father who came from a rich family who lived in a huge building that Rodrigo called a *castillo*. He had turned his back on a life of privilege for a life of piety and hardship, without the luxuries he had been used to all of his life. Like all of his companions he had few personal possessions and took a vow of poverty, chastity and obedience. It took quite a while to explain it all to Jabuti but with Rodrigo's endless patience he began to understand. Rodrigo saw the excitement in his eyes as he explained to Jabuti a world and a society in which Rodrigo was so passionate about.

One evening Rodrigo arranged a fine dinner for everyone in the village, with Jabuti and Mapi seated at the head of the table which was placed in the middle of the courtyard. Unfortunately Wanadi was absent as he was still too weak to join them.

'Who are all these other people?' Jabuti asked, looking around at all the other members of the community who had joined them.

'They are people of your country, they have come from many tribes from far away. They have become believers and it is my duty to educate and nurture them. I have sent two of my brothers out into the forest to continue to teach the word of our God.'

'You have brothers with you?' Mapi asked.

'No Mapi that is what we call them, they are like family to me though. I am what we call a *sacerdote*, I also went out on missions into the forest but I am getting too old now, so I stay here to look after everyone's well-being,' he said to them. 'I will show you later how much they have learned since they have come to live here.'

Jabuti was intrigued and continued eating his meal and carried on talking with Rodrigo. When the meal was complete the dishes were cleared away and then several of the children lined up at the end of the courtyard in their crisp white uniforms. Behind them stood numerous older children who held objects under their chins with long handles, and what looked to Jabuti like an arrow poised just above it. On cue from Roberto and in perfect sequence the children started singing so sweetly it brought tears to Jabuti and Mapi's eyes. Jabuti was startled and moved also by the sound which came from the musical instruments of a kind he had never seen before. They listened enraptured by the melody which echoed from the tree tops and filled the air with a pleasant vibration.

'That's how it makes me feel every time,' Rodrigo said as he turned to look at Jabuti and Mapi who sat visibly moved. 'I see your friend Wanadi is getting stronger day by day,' Rodrigo mentioned after the children had drifted away.

'Yes, with thanks to you Rodrigo,' Jabuti said.

'You are all welcome to stay here once Wanadi becomes well, I would very much like that.'

'Thank you Rodrigo but I could never believe in your God,' Jabuti replied, touched by his kind offer.

'We have families waiting back home for us…' Mapi said. 'I'm sorry Jabuti I wasn't thinking.'

'It's alright Mapi.'

'What will you do then? You have come so far.'

'How far away is your land?' Jabuti asked.

'It is a long way away from here, it would take many moons to reach my land. It is a very dangerous voyage,' Rodrigo answered. 'Why do you ask my child?'

'I wish to follow my father to this land you call *España*.'

'No Jabuti!' Mapi shouted out, horrified.

'Jabuti, I admire your courage but I don't think you really know what you are saying,' Rodrigo said.

'Why?'

'Listen to him Jabuti,' Mapi advised.

'You don't speak our language, the journey is a long and dangerous one and you have no way to support yourself.'

'Will this help?' Jabuti asked, unwrapping the object the white men called *oro*.

'Where did you get that?' Rodrigo asked incredulously.

Jabuti hadn't mentioned the *oro* that they had brought with them for fear of meeting other white men such as Diego; but Jabuti felt safe enough in Rodrigo's company to show him. Jabuti then recounted the story of meeting the white men and told him the full story.

'Be careful Jabuti, men would kill for an object such as that,' Rodrigo warned.

'I know, we have seen it with our own eyes,' Jabuti replied.

'Jabuti, think about what you are saying,' Mapi said. 'You have Maru waiting back home for you.'

'I know Mapi, but if I turn back now then what would I have achieved?' he asked, smiling warmly at his friend. 'I know that if I return and set eyes on my beloved Maru then I will never have the courage to leave her side again.'

'No Jabuti, I need to talk to Wanadi when he is awake,' Mapi said with a look of desperation. 'I know he'll agree with me.'

'You are a dear friend Mapi.'

'I see you are very head-strong Jabuti, can I not talk you out o—' Rodrigo began to say.

'Give me that *oro*!' came a menacing voice, cutting Rodrigo off in mid-sentence.

'Diego!' Jabuti and Mapi shouted out in unison.

They stood shocked as they looked at him standing in ragged clothes, with cuts and grazes on every part of his body. He was virtually unrecognisable in his bedraggled state, but through the dirt and grime Jabuti noticed his threatening and menacing stare. He stood facing them with the weapon that had wounded Mapi and the smaller ones firmly tied back around his waist.

'What is this, who is this man?' Rodrigo asked, shocked at the sudden intrusion into the peace of his village.

'He is the man I told you about,' Jabuti said, eyeing up Diego nervously.

'*Qué p*—?' Rodrigo started to say to Diego.

'*Cálla sacerdote*!' he hissed at Rodrigo.

'Wanadi was right,' Mapi whispered to Jabuti.

'That *oro* mine, you give now,' he said and Jabuti heard something click on the weapon he held.

'Jabuti, be very careful of this man,' Rodrigo warned him.

'*No te lo digo otra vez sacerdote!*' Diego screamed as he fired his weapon at Rodrigo's feet.

He dropped the smoking weapon and in one swift moment he pulled the two remaining ones from his waist belt and held them pointing in Jabuti's direction. Fearing for his life Jabuti reached underneath the table for the object that Diego so desired. Diego screamed at him as he was doing so and he fired at Jabuti's head, missing him by a fraction.

'Stop, wh—' he heard Diego start to say above the deafening roar.

His words ended abruptly in a spout of blood and spittle as he held the end of a spear which had entered into his neck and through to the other side. His eyes grew wide in alarm as he gasped for breath and continued clutching and grasping it in a futile attempt to ease his suffering. Diego tried to say something but all that he managed was a gurgling sound with red-coloured froth pouring from his mouth. Jabuti could no longer watch as Diego sank to his knees and looked up at him pleadingly, watching as his life's force ebbed away in front of his very eyes.

He and Mapi turned to see Wanadi leaning against one of the wooden crosses gasping and holding his stomach and grimacing in pain.

'I told you we should have taken his weapons,' he wheezed as Jabuti and Mapi rushed to his side.

Jabuti looked at him in concern at the pain he was in and felt intense sadness at what he had just been forced to do.

'He was going to use his weapon against you Jabuti,' Wanadi said.

'Thank you Wanadi, it's just that we have seen so much killing and because of me you have had to take another man's life.'

'I know that it is against our beliefs to take a life but I really think he was going to kill you; look how easily he took Alonso's life,' Wanadi replied.

'Wanadi speaks the truth Jabuti, even though killing is a sin in God's eyes I believe that sometimes you have to take a life to preserve life,' Rodrigo said, joining them.

'Is that what your God teaches you?' Jabuti asked.

'Well not exactly, but I have seen so much suffering since I have been here that I hold my own beliefs,' Rodrigo replied with a calm expression.

'What shall we do with him?' Mapi asked, looking towards Diego's battered and crumpled form.

'I will bury him alongside all the others who are resting in the *cementerio*,' Rodrigo said, carrying his body away with the help of several of the villagers.

'Jabuti wants to travel over the water with no end to find his father Wanadi,' Mapi said to Wanadi in desperation.

'I think it is the right thing for him to do Mapi.'

'But wh—'

'I know Mapi I'll miss him too,' he said to him. 'Have you really thought this through Jabuti?'

'No,' he laughed. 'But if I thought about it anymore then I fear I would not have the courage to leave.'

'I will come with you then,' Wanadi stated.

'Me too,' Mapi agreed.

'Ha!' Jabuti chuckled. 'Does this remind you of another time? No my friends, this time I have to go on my own,' he said, looking at his friends and trying hard to hold back his tears. 'My dear friends I can't allow it, I'm sorry; you have both suffered so much. You must go back to our village and tell them what has happened, otherwise they will fear that we are lost; or worse. Maru must know that I haven't forgotten about her and I will come back for her; if she will have me.'

CHAPTER TWENTY

'How are you feeling Wanadi?' Jabuti asked the next day as he visited him. Such was Wanadi's personality that he would only discuss issues when he was good and ready, and Jabuti had learned over the years not to pry too much.

'I'm fine Jabuti, you don't need to worry about me. Have you really thought about what you are doing?' he asked, deflecting the attention away from himself.

'I've had enough of thinking Wanadi, my head is tired. I just need to find some inner peace, and if it takes me across the water to find my father then that is what I will do.'

'I understand Jabuti, but we have been lucky to survive this journey so far. Why don't we just return home? No one will think any the less of you my friend.'

'I can't go back Wanadi until I have seen this through. I have to go whilst I still have the courage.'

'But I don't understand why you are trying to find a father you have never even known. I'm worried you will be disappointed.'

'So am I, but you have a father and a mother. It's no fault of yours, but you'll never know the feeling of emptiness and longing I have suffered all of my life. It's like a dull throbbing pain in my body that never leaves me, I'm tired of pretending Wanadi; I'm tired...' he said with such a look of sadness in his eyes that it brought Wanadi to tears.

'I don't think I really knew until today how much it has affected you Jabuti. I really feel for you, please let me come with you,' he pleaded.

'Oh Wanadi I would like nothing better, but what about Mapi? He can't go back on his own.'

'Talk with Rodrigo, he is a wise man,' Wanadi suggested.

Jabuti took his advice and sought an audience with Rodrigo, whilst Wanadi limped from his bed to go in search of Mapi to keep him company. As usual Jabuti found Rodrigo inside his house of worship, whereupon he smiled at Jabuti and asked him to join him on one of the pews.

'How is Wanadi?' Rodrigo asked.

'He is a strong man Rodrigo, he won't say anything about the killing of Diego until he is ready; or ever. I don't need to worry about him, it's Mapi who I am most concerned about,' Jabuti mentioned as he told him of his conversation with Wanadi.

'It is wise to have company Jabuti.'

'But what about Mapi? He can't return home alone, but I don't want to put him in more danger by taking him with me.'

'I will ask brothers Hernando and Luis to take Mapi back home. They should be returning soon, God willing.'

'But is that fair to them?'

'It is our calling Jabuti to spread the word of God, they will be delighted to help, I know.'

'Thank you Rodrigo but how will I tell Mapi? I fear he will feel abandoned.'

'From what I know of him Jabuti he will understand. Yes he will be upset, but if he really is a true friend then he'll have your best interests at heart.'

Thanking Rodrigo for his words of advice Jabuti went in search of Mapi, with a feeling of dread in his stomach. He saw Wanadi and Mapi sitting under the shade of a large tree where they were laughing and joking. As he walked towards them he felt sick to the the pit of his stomach at what he was about to tell Mapi.

At the last moment he lurched away, suddenly feeling selfish for taking Wanadi away with him. The enormity of what he was about to embark upon hit him with full intensity and he wandered around the village not able to settle anywhere. He soon found himself entering the peaceful garden of crosses, where he walked up to where his mother lay and sat down reverentially in front of her simple grave.

'Oh mother why did you have to leave me, why must I make all these decisions all on my own? If only I could have spoken with you, to tell you how I feel and what I am thinking,' he said, feeling a little self-conscious talking to a wooden cross. 'I would give anything to be given some advice, but it is my duty to shoulder this burden all on my own. I hope you would be proud of me mother,' he said and gently patted the lush grass below the cross.

He felt calm sitting amongst the crosses in the cooling shadow of the house of worship and for the first time since leaving home he was able to just sit and contemplate. Amongst the serenity of his surroundings he slowly came to the realisation that what he was about to do was futile and dangerous. With Maru waiting back home for him and having to break the dreadful news to Mapi it became all too much for Jabuti. With a sense of finality he decided to tell his friends that he would be going back home after all.

'I knew I'd find you here,' Mapi said as he walked into view.

'Mapi,' Jabuti said, smiling at him, 'I was just coming to find you.'

'You're going to find your father with Wanadi aren't you?'

'Oh Mapi, I was just coming to tell you th—'

'It's fine Jabuti, I think it is for the best,' he said with a smile.

'But I was just coming to tell you I've changed my mind, I'm not going now.'

'To come all this way and turn back? I don't think so Jabuti.'

'But how did you know what I was going to do, did Wanadi say anything?'

'He didn't need to tell me Jabuti, I knew you had been speaking with each other and afterwards he was just trying too hard with me, you know what he's like,' he said as they both shared a wry smile.

'I didn't know how to tell you Mapi, I came here to think about what to say. You think I should go then?'

'I want you to be happy Jabuti, and if that means I have to return home without you and Wanadi, then that's how it will be.'

'Your generosity humbles me Mapi.'

'I fear I might have been too hasty with my decisions again,' Jabuti mentioned to Rodrigo as they sat down together, some days later. 'I don't even know how to reach your homeland, or even how to find my father.'

'We came by what we call a *barco* Jabuti, it takes many, many moons to get to where I come from. When you arrive ask for brother Francisco, he will help you find your father and he will be glad to help,' Rodrigo replied. 'I don't even know when the next *barco* will arrive though Jabuti. I fear you may be staying with us for a while after all.'

'Well, that will give me time to learn your language Rodrigo,' Jabuti said. 'Tell me more about this *barco* you came in.'

'You pick up our language easily Jabuti, I see you will be a good student.' He smiled at this compliment and Rodrigo continued to tell him of his journey to Jabuti's land.

Jabuti listened enthralled as Rodrigo regaled him with a story of a ship many, many times bigger than their bongo which held a large crew of sailors and officers. Jabuti was shocked as Rodrigo told him of the punishments meted out in order to keep discipline onboard. Jabuti questioned his decision as he heard him tell of men tied to the mast and whipped on bare skin for minor infractions. Rodrigo said that they had to eat basic foodstuffs crawling with lice and weevils, soaked with the urine and faeces of rats and mice.

Feeling the need to let Jabuti know everything that could happen to him he told him of storms so violent in their intensity that men were thrown bodily from their bunks, and landing in pools of vomit that swished around below decks from the terrible sea sickness.

'Why would you go through such a voyage like that?' Jabuti asked of Rodrigo.

'For the same reason you seek your father Jabuti,' he said smiling. 'I came to spread the word of my God, he kept me safe and guided me through the hard times.'

'Shall I give these men you speak of this *oro* to help us on this voyage?'

'No Jabuti, you must keep it well hidden until you reach your destination. These are very hard men you will be travelling with, they would kill you just to hold it in their hands. I will arrange everything for you, you might need to work for your keep but that is all.'

'So what do we do now?'

'Well, we wait for brothers Hernando and Luis to return and then I will tell them of their next mission.'

'You are very kind Rodrigo.'

Brother's Hernando and Luis did indeed return, but not for several weeks later. They stumbled into the camp late one evening, tired and dirty from their travels, but as soon as they saw Rodrigo their eyes lit up and they embraced each other. Rodrigo introduced them to Jabuti and his friends and they accepted them as warmly as Rodrigo had done.

Hernando reminded Jabuti a little of Alonso for he had a kindly face and the same portly countenance. He had thick eyebrows which hid beneath a pair of kindly and inquisitive eyes, and Jabuti felt confident entrusting his friend's safety to him. Luis was tall and wiry with a hooked nose and a slightly nervous way of speaking, but Jabuti could tell that he had a ready sense of humour in the way that he made his friends laugh. They couldn't speak Jabuti's language as well as Rodrigo, so he translated for them all. Rodrigo informed Jabuti that they were eager and more than ready to accompany Mapi back to his village, but Jabuti asked that they be given more time to rest after their recent hardships.

Jabuti was really stalling for time though for he wasn't ready to face the day when he had to say goodbye to his good friend. He felt sad that once the brothers had recuperated then Mapi would be on his way, and Jabuti wasn't sure when he would next see him again.

The next week was intense for the three friends as they tried to come to terms with what they had been through and contemplating what was coming up next for them. Like an unstoppable force the days seemed to race by up to the evening before Mapi's departure. Jabuti tried to convince Mapi to stay a bit longer but such was Mapi's conviction that he insisted on leaving the next day, saying he would find it too hard otherwise.

Rodrigo helped prepare a simple meal of fish and manioc bread for the friends' last meal together and left them alone.

'So Mapi, do you like Hernando and Luis?' Jabuti asked.

'Yes, I think I do.'

'Good, so…er…do y—'

'Jabuti, just talk to me normally,' Mapi said, interrupting him, 'I'll be fine, stop worrying.'

'But I do Mapi, I feel really bad leaving you.'

'Jabuti, I have grown up a lot on this journey, or haven't you noticed?' he said with a smile. 'To tell you the truth I am a little tired and I really want to go back home now.'

'Really?'

'Yes really, Jabuti.'

Wanadi looked at Mapi and mouthed the words 'thank you' to him as Mapi gave him a wink in return.

'Wanadi, do you want to go b—?'

'Oh Jabuti, stop it, you're giving us all a headache!' Wanadi said as he pushed him playfully.

'Alright, alright,' he said laughing. 'I just want to make sure everyone is happy.'

'Jabuti, we want to make sure that you are happy,' Mapi said as Jabuti started to well up.

'There he goes again, spoiling another good evening,' Wanadi teased.

'Oh shut up,' Jabuti said and punched him in the shoulder as he dried his eyes.

Jabuti felt a deep sense of contentment for the first time in his life as he shared that last meal with his friends. As they laughed and joked he savoured every moment, from the pain in his ribs from laughing too much, to the genuine warmth between them as they told stories to each other.

Jabuti awoke early the next morning and took a walk alone along the pristine beach. He watched in fascination as crabs crawled out of their burrows, picking up various bits of food matter left behind from the constant ebb and flow of the ocean. He savoured the feel of the sand between his toes as it compressed beneath his feet. Looking back along the trail he had left he imagined that a kindly spirit followed behind on his footprints, looking out for him.

He sat down under the shade of a large palm tree and leaned back against it and stared out across the water. Whilst sitting there he noticed Mapi walking his way and smiled, watching him jump from each one of Jabuti's footsteps.

'Hello Jabuti,' Mapi said, walking up to him, 'I've caught you daydreaming again, I've never thought to ask you this before, but why do you spend so much time by the water?'

'I don't know Mapi,' Jabuti replied, motioning for Mapi to sit by his side. 'I suppose I feel like I can just let my mind wander when I'm close to water. It gives me a sense of inner peace which I can't find anywhere else. You know me well enough Mapi to understand that I need to get away from people and distractions every now and then.'

Mapi nodded and stared out to sea along with him, 'I wish that you find what you're looking for.'

'Thank you Mapi, I hope I find my father too.'

'I do as well, but I didn't mean that,' he said, turning to look at him. 'I hope you find the missing pieces in your life and I think you'll find what you are looking for deep within yourself. You are a very special person Jabuti, I just don't think you realise that as yet. You will find happiness either with or without your father.'

'Oh Mapi, you surprise me every day.'

'If you start crying I'll tell Wanadi,' Mapi said with a straight face as they both fell about laughing.

They walked back together to the village where they were met by Wanadi, who surprised them both by hugging Mapi and said, 'I'm really going to miss you my friend.' Despite himself, Wanadi couldn't help but shed a tear as he held onto him.

'Alright, alright, you're getting to be like Jabuti,' Mapi joked as he pushed him away. 'How are you two girls going to get by without me?'

Just then Rodrigo appeared and said to Mapi, 'Hernando and Luis are waiting for you, come find us when you are ready,' and he walked away, to give them time alone.

'Mapi, please tell Maru that I will return some day and if she'll still have me then I won't leave her side again,' Jabuti told him. 'Please be careful on your journey back, I'll be thinking about you always,' he said and embraced his friend one last time.

'Mapi, I know that I have always joked with you and made fun of you but I…' Wanadi trailed off, finding the emotion of the moment hard to deal with.

'I know Wanadi, I know,' Mapi replied with a brave smile. 'Look, I have to go now otherwise…well, you know.'

'Yes I do,' Jabuti said as he walked with him and Wanadi to find Hernando and Luis.

They found them waiting patiently in the courtyard and without wasting time Mapi picked up his backpack and walked with them to the edge of the compound. He walked towards the forest and stopped one last time to wave at his friends, and in an instant he was gone.

Jabuti put his arm around his friend's shoulder as they walked along the beach towards the same tree, where he had sat with Mapi. They stood underneath its cooling shade and gazed out across the water with no end, each lost in their own separate thoughts.

THE END

Made in the USA
San Bernardino, CA
25 March 2014